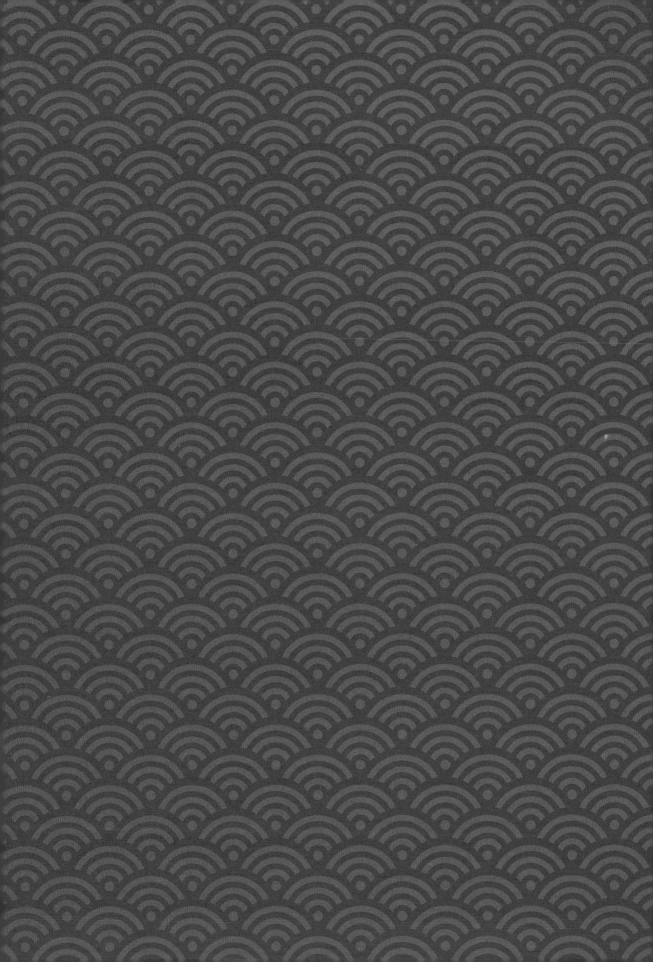

SUPERNATURAL TALES FROM
JAPAN

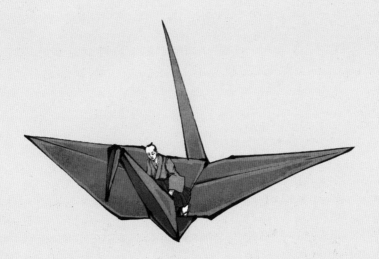

SUPERNATURAL TALES FROM

JAPAN

GHOSTS, GOBLINS, DEMONS AND MAGIC

Lafcadio Hearn

Yei Theodora Ozaki

ILLUSTRATIONS BY SAKYU

TUTTLE Publishing

Tokyo | Rutland, Vermont | Singapore

CONTENTS

THE STORY OF
MIMI NASHI HOICHI

More than seven hundred years ago, at Dan-no-ura, in the Straits of Shimonoseki, was fought the last battle of the long contest between the Heike, or Taira clan, and the Genji, or Minamoto clan. There the Heike perished utterly, with their women and children, and their infant emperor likewise—now remembered as Antoku Tenno. And that sea and shore have been haunted for seven hundred years... Elsewhere I told you about the strange crabs found there, called Heike crabs, which have human faces on their backs, and are said to be the spirits of the Heike warriors.[1] But there are many strange things to be seen and heard along that coast. On dark nights thousands of ghostly fires hover about the beach, or flit above the waves—pale lights which the fishermen call *oni-bi*, or demon fires; and, whenever the winds are up, a sound of great shouting comes from that sea, like a clamor of battle.

In former years the Heike were much more restless than they now are. They would rise about ships passing in the night, and try to sink them; and at all times they would watch for swimmers, to pull them down. It was in order to appease those dead that the Buddhist temple, Amidaji, was built at Akamagaseki.[2] A cemetery also was made close by, near the beach; and within it were set up monuments inscribed with the names of the drowned emperor and of his great vassals; and Buddhist services were regularly performed there, on behalf of the spirits of them. After the temple had been built, and the tombs erected, the Heike gave less trouble than before; but they continued to do queer things at intervals, proving that they had not found the perfect peace.

Some centuries ago there lived at Akamagaseki a blind man named Hoichi, who was famed for his skill in recitation and in playing upon the *biwa*.[3] From childhood he had been trained to recite and to play; and while yet a lad he had surpassed his teachers. As a professional *biwa-hoshi* he became famous chiefly by his recitations of the history of the Heike and the Genji; and it is said that when he sang the song of the battle of Dan-no-ura "even the goblins [*kijin*] could not refrain from tears."

At the outset of his career, Hoichi was very poor; but he found a good friend to help him. The priest of the Amidaji was fond of poetry and music; and he often invited Hoichi to the temple, to play and recite. Afterwards, being much impressed by the wonderful skill of the lad, the priest proposed that Hoichi should make the temple his home; and this offer was gratefully accepted. Hoichi was given a room in the temple building; and, in return for food and lodging, he was required only to gratify the priest with a musical performance on certain evenings, when otherwise disengaged.

One summer night the priest was called away, to perform a Buddhist service at the house of a dead parishioner; and he went there with his acolyte, leaving Hoichi alone in the temple. It was a hot night; and the blind man sought to cool himself on the veranda before his sleeping room. The veranda overlooked a small garden in the rear of the Amidaji. There Hoichi waited for the priest's return, and tried to relieve his solitude by practicing upon his *biwa*. Midnight passed; and the priest did not appear. But the atmosphere was still too warm for comfort within doors; and Hoichi remained outside. At last he heard steps approaching from the back gate. Somebody crossed the garden, advanced to the veranda, and halted directly in front of him—but it was not the priest. A deep voice called the blind man's name—abruptly and unceremoniously, in the manner of a samurai summoning an inferior:

"Hoichi!"

Hoichi was too much startled, for the moment, to respond; and the voice called again, in a tone of harsh command,

"Hoichi!"

"Hai!"[4] answered the blind man, frightened by the menace in the voice. "I am blind! I cannot know who calls!"

"There is nothing to fear," the stranger exclaimed, speaking more gently. "I am stopping near this temple, and have been sent to you with a message. My present lord, a person of exceedingly high rank, is now staying in Akamagaseki, with many noble attendants. He wished to view the scene of the battle of Dan-no-ura; and today he visited that place. Having heard of your skill in reciting the story of the battle, he now desires to hear your performance: so you will take your *biwa* and come with me at once to the house where the august assembly is waiting."

In those times, the order of a samurai was not to be lightly disobeyed. Hoichi donned his sandals, took his *biwa*, and went away with the stranger, who guided him deftly, but obliged him to walk very fast. The hand that guided was iron; and the clank of the warrior's stride proved him fully armed—probably some palace guard on duty. Hoichi's first alarm was over: he began to imagine himself in good luck; for, remembering the retainer's assurance about a "person of exceedingly high rank," he thought that the lord who wished to hear the recitation could not be less than a daimyo of the first class. Presently the samurai halted; and Hoichi became aware that they had arrived at a large gateway—and he wondered, for he could not remember any large gate in that part of the town, except the main gate of the Amidaji. "Kaimon!"[5] the samurai called, and there was a sound of unbarring; and the twain passed on. They traversed a space of garden, and halted again before some entrance; and the retainer cried in a loud voice, "Within there! I have brought Hoichi." Then came sounds of feet hurrying, and screens sliding, and rain doors opening, and voices of women in converse. By the language of the women Hoichi knew them to be domestics in some noble household; but he could not imagine to what place he had been conducted. Little time was allowed him for conjecture. After he had been helped to mount several stone steps, upon the last of which he was told to leave his sandals, a woman's hand guided him along interminable reaches of polished planking, and round pillared angles too many to remember, and over widths amazing of matted floor, into the middle of some vast apartment. There he thought that many great people were assembled: the sound of the rustling of silk was like the sound of leaves in a forest. He heard also a great humming of voices, talking in undertones; and the speech was the speech of courts.

Hoichi was told to put himself at ease, and he found a kneeling-cushion ready for him. After having taken his place upon it, and tuned his instrument, the voice of a woman—whom he divined to be the *rojo*, or matron in charge of the female service—addressed him, saying,

"It is now required that the history of the Heike be recited, to the accompaniment of the *biwa*."

Now the entire recital would have required a time of many nights: therefore Hoichi ventured a question:

"As the whole of the story is not soon told, what portion is it augustly desired that I now recite?"

The woman's voice made answer:

"Recite the story of the battle at Dan-no-ura—for the pity of it is the most deep."[6]

Then Hoichi lifted up his voice, and chanted the chant of the fight on the bitter sea, wonderfully making his *biwa* to sound like the straining of oars and the rushing of ships, the whirr and the hissing of arrows, the shouting and trampling of men, the crashing of steel upon helmets, the plunging of slain in the flood. And to left and right of him, in the pauses of his playing, he could hear voices murmuring praise: "How marvelous an artist!"—"Never in our own province was playing heard like this!"—"Not in all the empire is there another singer like Hoichi!" Then fresh courage came to him, and he played and sang yet better than before; and a hush of wonder deepened about him. But when at last he came to tell the fate of the fair and helpless—the piteous perishing of the women and children—and the death-leap of Nii-no-Ama, with the imperial infant in her arms—then all the listeners uttered together one long, long shuddering cry of anguish; and thereafter they wept and wailed so loudly and so wildly that the blind man was frightened by the violence and grief that he had made. For much time the sobbing and the wailing continued. But gradually the sounds of lamentation died away; and again, in the great stillness that followed, Hoichi heard the voice of the woman whom he supposed to be the *rojo*.

She said:

"Although we had been assured that you were a very skillful player upon the *biwa*, and without an equal in recitative, we did not know that anyone could be so skillful as you have proved yourself tonight. Our lord has been pleased to say that he intends to bestow upon you a fitting reward. But he desires that you shall perform before him once every night for the next six nights—after which time he will probably make his august return journey. Tomorrow night, therefore, you are to come here at the same hour. The retainer who tonight conducted you will be sent for you... There is another matter about which I have been ordered to inform you. It is required that you shall speak to no one of your visits here, during the time of our lord's august sojourn at Akamagaseki. As he is traveling incognito,[7] he commands that no mention of these things be made... You are now free to go back to your temple."

After Hoichi had duly expressed his thanks, a woman's hand conducted him to the entrance of the house, where the same retainer, who had before guided him, was waiting to take him home. The retainer led him to the veranda at the rear of the temple, and there bade him farewell.

It was almost dawn when Hoichi returned; but his absence from the temple had not been observed, as the priest, coming back at a very late hour, had supposed him asleep. During the day Hoichi was able to take some rest; and he said nothing about his strange adventure. In the middle of the following night the samurai again came for him, and led him to the august assembly, where he gave another recitation with the same success that had attended his previous performance. But during this second visit his absence from the temple was accidentally discovered; and after his return in the morning he was summoned to the presence of the priest, who said to him, in a tone of kindly reproach:

"We have been very anxious about you, friend Hoichi. To go out, blind and alone, at so late an hour, is dangerous. Why did you go without telling us? I could have ordered a servant to accompany you. And where have you been?"

Hoichi answered, evasively,

"Pardon me kind friend! I had to attend to some private business; and I could not arrange the matter at any other hour."

The priest was surprised, rather than pained, by Hoichi's reticence: he felt it to be unnatural, and suspected something wrong. He feared that the blind lad had been bewitched or deluded by some evil spirits. He did not ask any more questions; but he privately instructed the men servants of the temple to keep watch upon Hoichi's movements, and to follow him in case that he should again leave the temple after dark.

On the very next night, Hoichi was seen to leave the temple; and the servants immediately lighted their lanterns, and followed after him. But it was a rainy night, and very dark; and before the temple folks could get to the roadway, Hoichi had disappeared. Evidently he had walked very fast—a strange thing, considering his blindness; for the road was in a bad condition. The men hurried through the streets, making inquiries at every house which Hoichi was accustomed to visit; but nobody could give them any news of him. At last, as they were returning to the temple by way of the shore, they were startled by the sound of a *biwa*, furiously played, in the cemetery of the Amidaji. Except for some ghostly fires—such as usually flitted there on dark nights—all was blackness in that direction. But the men at once hastened to the cemetery; and there, by the help of their lanterns, they discovered Hoichi, sitting alone in the rain before the memorial tomb of Antoku Tenno, making his *biwa* resound, and loudly chanting the chant of the battle of Dan-no-ura. And behind him, and about him, and everywhere above the tombs, the fires of the dead were burning, like candles. Never before had so great a host of *oni-bi* appeared in the sight of mortal man...

"Hoichi San! Hoichi San!" the servants cried, "you are bewitched!... Hoichi San!"

But the blind man did not seem to hear. Strenuously he made his *biwa* to rattle and ring and clang; more and more wildly he chanted the chant of the battle of Dan-no-ura. They caught hold of him; they shouted into his ear,

"Hoichi San! Hoichi San! Come home with us at once!"

Reprovingly he spoke to them:

"To interrupt me in such a manner, before this august assembly, will not be tolerated."

Whereat, in spite of the weirdness of the thing, the servants could not help laughing. Sure that he had been bewitched, they now seized him, and pulled him up on his feet, and by main force hurried him back to the temple, where he was immediately relieved of his wet clothes, by order of the priest. Then the priest insisted upon a full explanation of his friend's astonishing behavior.

Hoichi long hesitated to speak. But at last, finding that his conduct had really alarmed and angered the good priest, he decided to abandon his reserve; and he related everything that had happened from the time of first visit of the samurai.

The priest said:

"Hoichi, my poor friend, you are now in great danger! How unfortunate that you did not tell me all this before! Your wonderful skill in music has indeed brought you into strange trouble. By this time you must be aware that you have not been visiting any house whatever, but have been passing your nights in the cemetery, among the tombs of the Heike; and it was before the memorial tomb of Antoku Tenno that our people tonight found you, sitting in the rain. All that you have been imagining was illusion—except the calling of the dead. By once obeying them, you have put yourself in their power. If you obey them again, after what has already occurred, they will tear you in pieces. But they would have destroyed you, sooner or later, in any event… Now I shall not be able to remain with you tonight: I am called away to perform another service. But, before I go, it will be necessary to protect your body by writing holy texts upon it."

Before sundown the priest and his acolyte stripped Hoichi: then, with their writing brushes, they traced upon his breast and back, head and face and neck, limbs and hands and feet—even upon the soles of his feet, and upon all parts of his body—the text of the holy sutra called *Hannya-Shin-Kyo*.[8] When this had been done, the priest instructed Hoichi, saying:

"Tonight, as soon as I go away, you must seat yourself on the veranda, and wait. You will be called. But, whatever may happen, do not answer, and do not move. Say nothing and sit still—as if meditating. If you stir, or make any noise, you will be torn asunder. Do not get frightened; and do not think of calling for help—because no help could save you. If you do exactly as I tell you, the danger will pass, and you will have nothing more to fear."

After dark the priest and the acolyte went away; and Hoichi seated himself on the veranda, according to the instructions given him. He laid his *biwa* on the planking beside him, and, assuming the attitude of meditation, remained quite still, taking care not to cough, or to breathe audibly. For hours he stayed thus.

Then, from the roadway, he heard the steps coming. They passed the gate, crossed the garden, approached the veranda, stopped—directly in front of him.

"Hoichi!" the deep voice called. But the blind man held his breath, and sat motionless.

"Hoichi!" grimly called the voice a second time. Then a third time—savagely: "Hoichi!"

Hoichi remained as still as a stone, and the voice grumbled:

"No answer! That won't do… Must see where the fellow is."

There was a noise of heavy feet mounting upon the veranda. The feet approached deliberately, halted beside him. Then, for long minutes, during which Hoichi felt his whole body shake to the beating of his heart, there was dead silence.

At last the gruff voice muttered close to him:

"Here is the *biwa*; but of the *biwa* player I see—only two ears! So that explains why he did not answer: he had no mouth to answer with—there is nothing left of him but his ears… Now to my lord those ears I will take—in proof that the august commands have been obeyed, so far as was possible."

At that instant Hoichi felt his ears gripped by fingers of iron, and torn off! Great as the pain was, he gave no cry. The heavy footfalls receded along the veranda, descended into the garden, passed out to the roadway, ceased. From either side of his head, the blind man felt a thick warm trickling; but he dared not lift his hands…

Before sunrise the priest came back. He hastened at once to the veranda in the rear, stepped and slipped upon something clammy, and uttered a cry of horror; for he saw, by the light of his lantern, that the clamminess was blood. But he perceived Hoichi sitting there, in the attitude of meditation—with the blood still oozing from his wounds.

"My poor Hoichi!" cried the startled priest, "what is this… You have been hurt?"

At the sound of his friend's voice, the blind man felt safe. He burst out sobbing, and tearfully told his adventure of the night.

"Poor, poor Hoichi!" the priest exclaimed, "all my fault! My very grievous fault! Everywhere upon your body the holy texts had been written—except upon your ears! I trusted my acolyte to do that part of the work; and it was very, very wrong of me not to have made sure that he had done it! Well, the matter cannot now be helped; we can only try to heal your hurts as soon as possible… Cheer up, friend! The danger is now well over. You will never again be troubled by those visitors."

With the aid of a good doctor, Hoichi soon recovered from his injuries. The story of his strange adventure spread far and wide, and soon made him famous. Many noble persons went to Akamagaseki to hear him recite; and large presents of money were given to him, so that he became a wealthy man... But from the time of his adventure, he was known only by the appellation of *Mimi Nashi Hoichi*: "Hoichi the Earless."

Notes

1. See Lafcadio Hearn's book *Kotto* for a description of these curious crabs.
2. Or, Shimonoseki. The town is also known by the name of Bakkan.
3. The *biwa*, a kind of four-stringed lute, is chiefly used in musical recitative. Formerly the professional minstrels who recited the *Heike Monogatari*, and other tragical histories, were called *biwa-hoshi*, or "lute-priests." The origin of this appellation is not clear; but it is possible that it may have been suggested by the fact that "lute-priests" as well as blind shampooers, had their heads shaven, like Buddhist priests. The *biwa* is played with a kind of plectrum, called *bachi*, usually made of horn.
4. A response to show that one has heard and is listening attentively.
5. A respectful term, signifying the opening of a gate. It was used by samurai when calling to the guards on duty at a lord's gate for admission.
6. Or the phrase might be rendered, "for the pity of that part is the deepest." The Japanese word for pity in the original text is "*aware.*"
7. "Traveling incognito" is at least the meaning of the original phrase, "making a disguised august-journey" (*shinobi no go-ryoko*).
8. The Smaller Pragña-Pâramitâ-Hridaya-Sûtra is thus called in Japanese. Both the smaller and larger sutras called Pragña-Pâramitâ ("Transcendent Wisdom") have been translated by the late Professor Max Müller, and can be found in volume xlix of the *Sacred Books of the East* ("Buddhist Mahayana Sutras"). Apropos of the magical use of the text, as described in this story, it is worth remarking that the subject of the sutra is the Doctrine of the Emptiness of Forms, that is to say, of the unreal character of all phenomena or noumena... "Form is emptiness; and emptiness is form. Emptiness is not different from form; form is not different from emptiness. What is form—that is emptiness. What is emptiness—that is form... Perception, name, concept, and knowledge, are also emptiness... There is no eye, ear, nose, tongue, body, and mind... But when the envelopment of consciousness has been annihilated, then he [*the seeker*] becomes free from all fear, and beyond the reach of change, enjoying final Nirvana."

How an Old Man Lost His Wen

Many, many years ago there lived a good old man who had a wen like a tennis ball growing out of his right cheek. This lump was a great disfigurement to the old man, and so annoyed him that for many years he spent all his time and money in trying to get rid of it. He tried everything he could think of. He consulted many doctors far and near, and took all kinds of medicines both internally and externally. But it was all of no use. The lump only grew bigger and bigger till it was nearly as big as his face, and in despair he gave up all hopes of ever losing it, and resigned himself to the thought of having to carry the lump on his face all his life.

One day the firewood gave out in his kitchen, so, as his wife wanted some at once, the old man took his ax and set out for the woods up among the hills not very far from his home. It was a fine day in the early autumn, and the old man enjoyed the fresh air and was in no hurry to get home. So the whole afternoon passed quickly while he was chopping wood, and he had collected a goodly pile to take back to his wife. When the day began to draw to a close, he turned his face homewards.

The old man had not gone far on his way down the mountain pass when the sky clouded and rain began to fall heavily. He looked about for some shelter, but there was not even a charcoal burner's hut near. At last he espied a large hole in the hollow trunk of a tree. The hole was near the ground, so he crept in easily, and sat down in hopes that he had only been overtaken by a mountain shower, and that the weather would soon clear.

But much to the old man's disappointment, instead of clearing the rain fell more and more heavily, and finally a heavy thunderstorm broke over the mountain. The thunder roared so terrifically, and the heavens seemed to be so ablaze with lightning, that the old man could hardly believe himself to be alive. He thought that he must die of fright. At last, however, the sky cleared, and the whole country was aglow in the rays of the setting sun. The old man's spirits revived when he looked out at the beautiful twilight, and he was about to step out from his strange hiding place in the hollow tree when the sound of what seemed like the approaching steps of several people caught his ear. He at once thought that his friends had come to look for him, and he was delighted at the idea of having some jolly companions with whom to walk home. But on looking out from the tree, what was his amazement to see, not his friends, but hundreds of demons coming towards the spot. The more he looked, the greater was his astonishment. Some of these demons were as large as giants, others had great big eyes out of all proportion to the rest of their bodies, others again had absurdly long noses, and some had such big mouths that they seemed to open from ear to ear. All had horns growing on their foreheads. The old man was so surprised at what he saw that he lost his balance and fell out of the hollow tree. Fortunately for him the demons did not see him, as the tree was in the background. So he picked himself up and crept back into the tree.

While he was sitting there and wondering impatiently when he would be able to get home, he heard the sounds of gay music, and then some of the demons began to sing.

"What are these creatures doing?" said the old man to himself. "I will look out, it sounds very amusing."

On peeping out, the old man saw that the demon chief himself was actually sitting with his back against the tree in which he had taken refuge, and all the other demons were sitting round, some drinking and some dancing. Food and wine was spread before them on the ground, and the demons were evidently having a great entertainment and enjoying themselves immensely.

It made the old man laugh to see their strange antics.

"How amusing this is!" laughed the old man to himself "I am now quite old, but I have never seen anything so strange in all my life."

He was so interested and excited in watching all that the demons were doing, that he forgot himself and stepped out of the tree and stood looking on.

The demon chief was just taking a big cup of Sake and watching one of the demons dancing. In a little while he said with a bored air:

"Your dance is rather monotonous. I am tired of watching it. Isn't there any one amongst you all who can dance better than this fellow?"

Now the old man had been fond of dancing all his life, and was quite an expert in the art, and he knew that he could do much better than the demon.

"Shall I go and dance before these demons and let them see what a human being can do? It may be dangerous, for if I don't please them they may kill me!" said the old fellow to himself.

His fears, however, were soon overcome by his love of dancing. In a few minutes he could restrain himself no longer, and came out before the whole party of demons and began to dance at once. The old man, realizing that his life probably depended on whether he pleased these strange creatures or not, exerted his skill and wit to the utmost.

The demons were at first very surprised to see a man so fearlessly taking part in their entertainment, and then their surprise soon gave place to admiration.

"How strange!" exclaimed the horned chief. "I never saw such a skillful dancer before! He dances admirably!"

When the old man had finished his dance, the big demon said:

"Thank you very much for your amusing dance. Now give us the pleasure of drinking a cup of wine with us," and with these words he handed him his largest wine cup.

The old man thanked him very humbly:

"I did not expect such kindness from your lordship. I fear I have only disturbed your pleasant party by my unskillful dancing."

"No, no," answered the big demon. "You must come often and dance for us. Your skill has given us much pleasure."

The old man thanked him again and promised to do so.

"Then will you come again tomorrow, old man?" asked the demon.

"Certainly, I will," answered the old man.

"Then you must leave some pledge of your word with us," said the demon.

"Whatever you like," said the old man.

"Now what is the best thing he can leave with us as a pledge?" asked the demon, looking round.

Then said one of the demon's attendants kneeling behind the chief:

"The token he leaves with us must be the most important thing to him in his possession. I see the old man has a wen on his right cheek. Now mortal men consider such a wen very fortunate. Let my lord take the lump from the old man's right cheek, and he will surely come tomorrow, if only to get that back."

"You are very clever," said the demon chief, giving his horns an approving nod. Then he stretched out a hairy arm and claw-like hand, and took the great lump from the old man's right cheek. Strange to say, it came off as easily as a ripe plum from the tree at the demon's touch, and then the merry troop of demons suddenly vanished.

The old man was lost in bewilderment by all that had happened. He hardly knew for some time where he was. When he came to understand what had happened to him, he was delighted to find that the lump on his face, which had for so many years disfigured him, had really been taken away without any pain to himself. He put up his hand to feel if any scar remained, but found that his right cheek was as smooth as his left.

The sun had long set, and the young moon had risen like a silver crescent in the sky. The old man suddenly realized how late it was and began to hurry home. He patted his right cheek all the time, as if to make sure of his good fortune in having lost the wen. He was so happy that he found it impossible to walk quietly—he ran and danced the whole way home.

He found his wife very anxious, wondering what had happened to make him so late. He soon told her all that had passed since he left home that afternoon. She was quite as happy as her husband when he showed her that the ugly lump had disappeared from his face, for in her youth she had prided herself on his good looks, and it had been a daily grief to her to see the horrid growth.

Now next door to this good old couple there lived a wicked and disagreeable old man. He, too, had for many years been troubled with the growth of a wen on his left cheek, and he, too, had tried all manner of things to get rid of it, but in vain.

He heard at once, through the servant, of his neighbor's good luck in losing the lump on his face, so he called that very evening and asked his friend to tell him everything that concerned the loss of it. The good old man told his disagreeable neighbor all that had happened to him. He described the place where he would find the hollow tree in which to hide, and advised him to be on the spot in the late afternoon towards the time of sunset.

The old neighbor started out the very next afternoon, and after hunting about for some time, came to the hollow tree just as his friend had described. Here he hid himself and waited for the twilight.

Just as he had been told, the band of demons came at that hour and held a feast with dance and song. When this had gone on for some time the chief of the demons looked around and said:

"It is now time for the old man to come as he promised us. Why doesn't he come?"

When the second old man heard these words he ran out of his hiding place in the tree and, kneeling down before the *oni*, said:

"I have been waiting for a long time for you to speak!"

"Ah, you are the old man of yesterday," said the demon chief. "Thank you for coming, you must dance for us soon."

The old man now stood up and opened his fan and began to dance. But he had never learned to dance, and knew nothing about the necessary gestures and different positions. He thought that anything would please the demons, so he just hopped about, waving his arms and stamping his feet, imitating as well as he could any dancing he had ever seen.

The *oni* were very dissatisfied at this exhibition, and said amongst themselves:

"How badly he dances today!"

Then to the old man the demon chief said:

"Your performance today is quite different from the dance of yesterday. We don't wish to see any more of such dancing. We will give you back the pledge you left with us. You must go away at once."

With these words he took out from a fold of his dress the lump which he had taken from the face of the old man who had danced so well the day before, and threw it at the right cheek of the old man who stood before him. The lump immediately attached itself to his cheek as firmly as if it had grown there always, and all attempts to pull it off were useless. The wicked old man, instead of losing the lump on his left cheek as he had hoped, found to his dismay that he had but added another to his right cheek in his attempt to get rid of the first.

He put up first one hand and then the other to each side of his face to make sure if he were not dreaming a horrible nightmare. No, sure enough there was now a great wen on the right side of his face as on the left. The demons had all disappeared, and there was nothing for him to do but to return home. He was a pitiful sight, for his face, with the two large lumps, one on each side, looked just like a Japanese gourd.

THE BOY WHO
DREW CATS

A long, long time ago, in a small country village in Japan, there lived a poor farmer and his wife, who were very good people. They had a number of children, and found it very hard to feed them all. The elder son was strong enough when only fourteen years old to help his father; and the little girls learned to help their mother almost as soon as they could walk.

But the youngest child, a little boy, did not seem to be fit for hard work. He was very clever, cleverer than all his brothers and sisters; but he was quite weak and small, and people said he could never grow very big. So his parents thought it would be better for him to become a priest than to become a farmer. They took him with them to the village temple one day, and asked the good old priest who lived there, if he would have their little boy for his acolyte, and teach him all that a priest ought to know.

The old man spoke kindly to the lad, and asked him some hard questions. So clever were the answers that the priest agreed to take the little fellow into the temple as an acolyte, and to educate him for the priesthood.

The boy learned quickly what the old priest taught him, and was very obedient in most things. But he had one fault. He liked to draw cats during study hours, and to draw cats even where cats ought not to have been drawn at all.

Whenever he found himself alone, he drew cats. He drew them on the margins of the priest's books, and on all the screens of the temple, and on the walls, and on the pillars. Several times the priest told him this was not right; but he did not stop drawing cats. He drew them because he could not really help it. He had what is called "the genius of an artist," and just for that reason he was not quite fit to be an acolyte; a good acolyte should study books.

One day after he had drawn some very clever pictures of cats upon a paper screen, the old priest said to him severely: "My boy, you must go away from this temple at once. You will never make a good priest, but perhaps you will become a great artist. Now let me give you a last piece of advice, and be sure you never forget it. Avoid large places at night; keep to small!"

The boy did not know what the priest meant by saying, "Avoid large places; keep to small." He thought and thought, while he was tying up his little bundle of clothes to go away; but he could not understand those words, and he was afraid to speak to the priest anymore, except to say goodbye.

He left the temple very sorrowfully, and began to wonder what he should do. If he went straight home he felt sure his father would punish him for having been disobedient to the priest, so he was afraid to go home. All at once he remembered that at the next village, twelve miles away, there was a very big temple. He had heard there were several priests at that temple; and he made up his mind to go to them and ask them to take him for their acolyte.

Now that big temple was closed up but the boy did not know this fact. The reason it had been closed up was that a goblin had frightened the priests away, and had taken possession of the place. Some brave warriors had afterward gone to the temple at night to kill the goblin; but they had never been seen alive again. Nobody had ever told these things to the boy; so he walked all the way to the village hoping to be kindly treated by the priests!

When he got to the village it was already dark, and all the people were in bed, but he saw the big temple on a hill at the other end of the principal street, and he saw there was a light in the temple. People who tell the story say the goblin used to make that light, in order to tempt lonely travelers to ask for shelter. The boy went at once to the temple, and knocked. There was no sound inside. He knocked and knocked again; but still nobody came. At last he pushed gently at the door, and was quite glad to find that it had not been fastened. So he went in, and saw a lamp burning, but no priest.

He thought some priest would be sure to come very soon, and he sat down and waited. Then he noticed that everything in the temple was gray with dust, and thickly spun over with cobwebs. So he thought to himself that the priests would certainly like to have an acolyte, to keep the place clean. He wondered why they had allowed everything to get so dusty. What most pleased him, however, were some big white screens, good to paint cats upon. Though he was tired, he looked at once for a writing box, and found one, and ground some ink, and began to paint cats.

He painted a great many cats upon the screens; and then he began to feel very, very sleepy. He was just on the point of lying down to sleep beside one of the screens, when he suddenly remembered the words, "Avoid large places; keep to small!"

The temple was very large; he was all alone; and as he thought of these words, though he could not quite understand them, he began to feel for the first time a little afraid; and he resolved to look for a small place in which to sleep. He found a little cabinet, with a sliding door, and went into it, and shut himself up. Then he lay down and fell fast asleep.

Very late in the night he was awakened by a most terrible noise, a noise of fighting and screaming. It was so dreadful that he was afraid even to look through a chink of the little cabinet: he lay very still, holding his breath for fright.

The light that had been in the temple went out; but the awful sounds continued, and became more awful, and all the temple shook. After a long time silence came; but the boy was still afraid to move. He did not move until the light of the morning sun shone into the cabinet through the chinks of the little door.

Then he got out of his hiding place very cautiously, and looked about. The first thing he saw was that all the floor of the temple was covered with blood. And then he saw, lying dead in the middle of it, an enormous, monstrous rat—a goblin-rat—bigger than a cow!

But who or what could have killed it? There was no man or other creature to be seen. Suddenly the boy observed that the mouths of all the cats he had drawn the night before, were red and wet with blood. Then he knew that the goblin had been killed by the cats which he had drawn. And then also, for the first time, he understood why the wise old priest had said to him, "Avoid large places at night; keep to small."

Afterward that boy became a very famous artist. Some of the cats which he drew are still shown to travelers in Japan.

THE BADGER
HAUNTED TEMPLE

Once long ago, in southern Japan, in the town of Kumamoto, there lived a young samurai, who had a great devotion to the sport of fishing. Armed with his large basket and tackle, he would often start out in the early morning and pass the whole day at his favorite pastime, returning home only at nightfall.

One fine day he had more than usual luck. In the late afternoon, when he examined his basket, he found it full to overflowing. Highly delighted at his success, he wended his way homewards with a light heart, singing snatches of merry songs as he went along.

It was already dusk when he happened to pass a deserted Buddhist temple. He noticed that the gate stood half open, and hung loosely on its rusty hinges, and the whole place had a dilapidated and tumbledown appearance.

What was the young man's astonishment to see, in striking contrast to such a forlorn environment, a pretty young girl standing just within the gate.

As he approached she came forward, and looking at him with a meaningful glance, smiled, as if inviting him to enter into conversation. The samurai thought her manner somewhat strange, and at first was on his guard. Some mysterious influence, however, compelled him to stop, and he stood irresolutely admiring the fair young face, blooming like a flower in its somber setting.

When she noticed his hesitation she made a sign to him to approach. Her charm was so great and the smile with which she accompanied the gesture so irresistible, that half unconsciously, he went up the stone steps, passed through the semi-open portal, and entered the courtyard where she stood awaiting him.

The maiden bowed courteously, then turned and led the way up the stone-flagged pathway to the temple. The whole place was in the most woeful condition, and looked as if it had been abandoned for many years.

When they reached what had once been the priest's house, the samurai saw that the interior of the building was in a better state of preservation than the outside led one to suppose. Passing along the veranda into the front room, he noticed that the tatami were still presentable, and that a sixfold screen adorned the chamber.

The girl gracefully motioned her guest to sit down in the place of honor near the alcove.

"Does the priest of the temple live here?" asked the young man, seating himself.

"No," answered the girl, "there is no priest here now. My mother and I only came here yesterday. She has gone to the next village to buy some things and may not be able to come back tonight. But honorably rest awhile, and let me give you some refreshment."

The girl then went into the kitchen apparently to make the tea, but though the guest waited a long time, she never returned.

By this time the moon had risen, and shone so brightly into the room, that it was as light as day. The samurai began to wonder at the strange behavior of the damsel, who had inveigled him into such a place only to disappear and leave him in solitude.

Suddenly he was startled by someone sneezing loudly behind the screen. He turned his head in the direction from whence the sound came. To his utter amazement, not the pretty girl whom he had expected, but a huge, red-faced, bald-headed priest stalked out. He must have been about seven feet in height, for his head towered nearly to the ceiling, and he carried an iron wand, which he raised in a threatening manner.

"How dare you enter my house without my permission?" shouted the fierce-looking giant. "Unless you go away at once I will beat you into dust."

Frightened out of his wits, the young man took to his heels, and rushed with all speed out of the temple.

As he fled across the courtyard he heard peals of loud laughter behind him. Once outside the gate he stopped to listen, and still the strident laugh continued. Suddenly it occurred to him, that in the alarm of his hasty exit, he had forgotten his basket of fish. It was left behind in the temple. Great was his chagrin, for never before had he caught so much fish in a single day; but lacking the courage to go back and demand it, there was no alternative but to return home empty-handed.

The following day he related his strange experience to several of his friends. They were all highly amused at such an adventure, and some of them plainly intimated that the seductive maiden and the aggressive giant were merely hallucinations that owed their origin to the sake flask.

At last one man, who was a good fencer, said:

"Oh, you must have been deluded by a badger who coveted your fish. No one lives in that temple. It has been deserted ever since I can remember. I will go there this evening and put an end to his mischief."

He then went to a fishmonger, purchased a large basket of fish, and borrowed an angling rod. Thus equipped, he waited impatiently for the sun to set. When the dusk began to fall he buckled on his sword and set out for the temple, carefully shouldering his bait that was to lead to the undoing of the badger. He laughed confidently to himself as he said: "I will teach the old fellow a lesson!"

As he approached the ruin what was his surprise to see, not one, but three girls standing there.

"O, ho! that is the way the wind lies, is it, but the crafty old sinner won't find it such an easy matter to make a fool of me."

No sooner was he observed by the pretty trio than by gestures they invited him to enter. Without any hesitation, he followed them into the building, and boldly seated himself upon the mats. They placed the customary tea and cakes before him, and then brought in a flagon of wine and an extraordinarily large cup.

The swordsman partook neither of the tea nor the sake, and shrewdly watched the demeanor of the three maidens.

Noticing his avoidance of the proffered refreshment, the prettiest of them artlessly inquired:

"Why don't you take some sake?"

"I dislike both tea and sake," replied the valiant guest, "but if you have some accomplishment to entertain me with, if you can dance or sing, I shall be delighted to see you perform."

"Oh, what an old-fashioned man of propriety you are! If you don't drink, you surely know nothing of love either. What a dull existence yours must be! But we can dance a little, so if you will condescend to look, we shall be very pleased to try to amuse you with our performance, poor as it is."

The maidens then opened their fans and began to posture and dance. They exhibited so much skill and grace, however, that the swordsman was astonished, for it was unusual that country girls should be so deft and well trained. As he watched them he became more and more fascinated, and gradually lost sight of the object of his mission.

Lost in admiration, he followed their every step, their every movement, and as the Japanese storyteller says, he forgot himself entirely, entranced at the beauty of their dancing.

Suddenly he saw that the three performers had become *headless!* Utterly bewildered, he gazed at them intently to make sure that he was not dreaming. Lo! and behold! each was holding her own head in her hands. They then threw them up and caught them as they fell. Like children playing a game of ball, they tossed their heads from one to the other. At last the boldest of the three threw her head at the young fencer. It fell on his knees, looked up in his face, and laughed at him. Angered at the girl's impertinence, he cast the head back at her in disgust, and drawing his sword, made several attempts to cut down the goblin dancer as she glided to and fro playfully tossing up her head and catching it.

But she was too quick for him, and like lightning darted out of the reach of his sword.

"Why don't you catch me?" she jeered mockingly. Mortified at his failure, he made another desperate attempt, but once more she adroitly eluded him, and sprang up to the top of the screen.

"I am here! Can you not reach me this time?" and she laughed at him in derision.

Again he made a thrust at her, but she proved far too nimble for him, and again, for the third time, he was foiled.

Then the three girls tossed their heads on their respective necks, shook them at him, and with shouts of weird laughter they vanished from sight.

As the young man came to his senses he vaguely gazed around. Bright moonlight illumined the whole place, and the stillness of the midnight was unbroken save for the thin tinkling chirping of the insects. He shivered as he realized the lateness of the hour and the wild loneliness of that uncanny spot. His basket of fish was nowhere to be seen. He understood, that he, too, had come under the spell of the wizard-badger, and like his friend, at whom he had laughed so heartily the day before, he had been bewitched by the wily creature.

But, although deeply chagrined at having fallen such an easy dupe, he was powerless to take any sort of revenge. The best he could do was to accept his defeat and return home.

Among his friends there was a doctor, who was not only a brave man, but one full of resource. On hearing of the way the mortified swordsman had been bamboozled, he said:

"Now leave this to me. Within three days I will catch that old badger and punish him well for all his diabolical tricks."

The doctor went home and prepared a savory dish cooked with meat. Into this he mixed some deadly poison. He then cooked a second portion for himself. Taking these separate dishes and a bottle of sake with him, towards evening he set out for the ruined temple.

When he reached the mossy courtyard of the old building he found it solitary and deserted. Following the example of his friends, he made his way into the priest's room, intensely curious to see what might befall him, but, contrary to his expectation, all was empty and still. He knew that goblin-badgers were such crafty animals that it was almost impossible for anyone, however cautious, to be able to cope successfully with their snares and Fata Morganas. But he determined to be particularly wide awake and on his guard, so as not to fall a prey to any hallucination that the badger might raise.

The night was beautiful, and calm as the moldering tombs in the temple graveyard. The full moon shone brightly over the great black sloping roofs, and cast a flood of light into the room where the doctor was patiently awaiting the mysterious foe. The minutes went slowly by, an hour elapsed, and still no ghostly visitant appeared. At last the baffled intruder placed his flask of wine before him and began to make preparations for his evening meal, thinking that possibly the badger might be unable to resist the tempting savor of the food.

"There is nothing like solitude," he mused aloud. "What a perfect night it is! How lucky I am to have found this deserted temple from which to view the silvery glory of the autumn moon."

For some time he continued to eat and drink, smacking his lips like a country gourmet in enjoyment of the meal. He began to think that the badger, knowing that he had found his match at last, intended to leave him alone. Then to his delight, he heard the sound of footsteps. He watched the entrance to the room, expecting the old wizard to assume his favorite disguise, and that some pretty maiden would come to cast a spell upon him with her fascinations.

But, to his surprise, who should come into sight but an old priest, who dragged himself into the room with faltering steps and sank down upon the mats with a deep long-drawn sigh of weariness. Apparently between seventy and eighty years of age, his clothes were old and travel-stained, and in his withered hands he carried a rosary. The effort of ascending the steps had evidently been a great trial to him, he breathed heavily and seemed in a state of great exhaustion. His whole appearance was one to arouse pity in the heart of the beholder.

"May I inquire who are you?" asked the doctor.

The old man replied, in a quavering voice, "I am the priest who used to live here many years ago when the temple was in a prosperous condition. As a youth I received my training here under the abbot then in charge, having been dedicated from childhood to the service of the most holy Buddha by my parents. At the time of the great Saigo's rebellion I was sent to another parish. When the castle of Kumamoto was besieged, alas! my own temple was burned to the ground. For years I wandered from place to place and fell on very hard times. In my old age and misfortunes my heart at last yearned to come back to this temple, where I spent so many happy years as an acolyte. It is my hope to spend my last days here. You can imagine my grief when I found it utterly abandoned, sunk in decay, with no priest in charge to offer up the daily prayers to the Lord Buddha, or to keep up the rites for the dead buried here. It is now my sole desire to collect money and to restore the temple. But alas! age and illness and want of food have robbed me of my strength, and I fear that I shall never be able to achieve what I have planned," and here the old man broke down and shed tears—a pitiful sight.

When wiping his eyes with the sleeve of his threadbare robe, he looked hungrily at the food and wine on which the doctor was regaling himself, and added, wistfully:

"Ah, I see you have a delicious meal there and wine withal, which you are enjoying while gazing at the moonlit scenery. I pray you spare me a little, for it is many days since I have had a good meal and I am half famished."

At first the doctor was persuaded that the story was true, so plausible did it sound, and his heart was filled with compassion for the old bonze. He listened carefully till the melancholy recital was finished.

Then something in the accent of speech struck his ear as being different to that of a human being, and he reflected.

"This may be the badger! I must not allow myself to be deceived! The crafty cunning animal is planning to palm off his customary tricks on me, but he shall see that I am as clever as he is."

The doctor pretended to believe in the old man's story, and answered:

"Indeed, I deeply sympathize with your misfortunes. You are quite welcome to share my meal—nay, I will give you with pleasure all that is left, and, moreover, I promise to bring you some more tomorrow. I will also inform my friends and acquaintances of your pious plan to restore the temple, and will give all the assistance in my power in your work of collecting subscriptions." He then pushed forward the untouched plate of food which contained poison, rose from the mats, and took his leave, promising to return the next evening.

All the friends of the doctor who had heard him boast that he would outwit the badger, arrived early next morning, curious to know what had befallen him. Many of them were very sceptical regarding the tale of the badger trickster, and ascribed the illusions of their friends to the sake bottle.

The doctor would give no answer to their many inquiries, but merely invited them to accompany him.

"Come and see for yourselves," he said, and guided them to the old temple, the scene of so many uncanny experiences.

First of all they searched the room where he had sat the evening before, but nothing was to be found except the empty basket in which he had carried the food for himself and the badger. They investigated the whole place thoroughly, and at last, in one of the dark corners of the temple chamber, they came upon the dead body of an old, old badger. It was the size of a large dog, and its hair was gray with age. Everyone was convinced that it must be at least several hundred years old.

The doctor carried it home in triumph. For several days the people in the neighborhood came in large numbers to gloat over the hoary carcass, and to listen in awe and wonder to the marvelous stories of the numbers of people that had been duped and befooled by the magic powers of the old goblin-badger.

The writer adds that he was told another badger story concerning the same temple. Many of the old people in the parish remember the incident, and one of them related the following story.

Years before, when the sacred building was still in a prosperous state, the priest in charge celebrated a great Buddhist festival, which lasted some days. Amongst the numerous devotees who attended the services he noticed a very handsome youth, who listened with profound reverence, unusual in one so young, to the sermons and litanies. When the festival was over and the other worshippers had gone, he lingered around the temple as though loth to leave the sacred spot. The head priest, who had conceived a liking for the lad, judged from his refined and dignified appearance that he must be the son of a high-class samurai family, probably desirous of entering the priesthood.

Gratified by the youth's apparent religious fervor, the holy man invited him to come to his study, and thereupon gave him some instruction in the Buddhist doctrines. He listened with the utmost attention for the whole afternoon to the bonze's learned discourse, and thanked him repeatedly for the condescension and trouble he had taken in instructing one so unworthy as himself.

The afternoon waned and the hour for the evening meal came round. The priest ordered a bowl of macaroni to be brought for the visitor, who proved to be the owner of a phenomenal appetite, and consumed three times as much as a full-grown man.

He then bowed most courteously and asked permission to return home. In bidding him goodbye, the priest, who felt a curious fascination for the youth, presented him with a gold-lacquered medicine box (*inro*) as a parting souvenir.

The lad prostrated himself in gratitude, and then took his departure.

The next day the temple servant, sweeping the graveyard, came across a badger. He was quite dead, and was dressed in a straw covering put on in such a way as to resemble the clothes of a human being. To his side was tied a gold-lacquered *inro*, and his paunch was much distended and as round as a large bowl. It was evident that the creature's gluttony had been the cause of his death, and the priest, on seeing the animal, identified the *inro* as the one which he had bestowed upon the good-looking lad the day before, and knew that he had been the victim of a badger's deceiving wiles.

It was thus certain that the temple had been haunted by a pair of goblin-badgers, and that when this one had died, its mate had continued to inhabit the same temple even after it had been abandoned. The creature had evidently taken a fantastic delight in bewitching wayfarers and travelers, or anyone who carried delectable food with them, and while mystifying them with his tricks and illusions, had deftly abstracted their baskets and bundles, and had lived comfortably upon his stolen booty.

The Story of the Man Who Did Not Wish to Die

Long, long ago there lived a man called Sentaro. His surname meant "Millionaire," but although he was not so rich as all that, he was still very far removed from being poor. He had inherited a small fortune from his father and lived on this, spending his time carelessly, without any serious thoughts of work, till he was about thirty-two years of age.

One day, without any reason whatsoever, the thought of death and sickness came to him. The idea of falling ill or dying made him very wretched.

"I should like to live," he said to himself, "till I am five or six hundred years old at least, free from all sickness. The ordinary span of a man's life is very short."

He wondered whether it were possible, by living simply and frugally henceforth, to prolong his life as long as he wished.

He knew there were many stories in ancient history of emperors who had lived a thousand years, and there was a Princess of Yamato, who, it was said, lived to the age of five hundred. This was the latest story of a very long life record.

Sentaro had often heard the tale of the Chinese king named Shin-no-Shiko. He was one of the most able and powerful rulers in Chinese history. He built all the large palaces, and also the famous great wall of China. He had everything in the world he could wish for, but in spite of all his happiness and the luxury and the splendor of his Court, the wisdom of his councilors and the glory of his reign, he was miserable because he knew that one day he must die and leave it all.

When Shin-no-Shiko went to bed at night, when he rose in the morning, as he went through his day, the thought of death was always with him. He could not get away from it. Ah—if only he could find the Elixir of Life, he would be happy.

The Emperor at last called a meeting of his courtiers and asked them all if they could not find for him the Elixir of Life of which he had so often read and heard.

One old courtier, Jofuku by name, said that far away across the seas there was a country called Horaizan, and that certain hermits lived there who possessed the secret of the Elixir of Life. Whoever drank of this wonderful draught lived forever.

The Emperor ordered Jofuku to set out for the land of Horaizan, to find the hermits, and to bring him back a phial of the magic elixir. He gave Jofuku one of his best junks, fitted it out for him, and loaded it with great quantities of treasures and precious stones for Jofuku to take as presents to the hermits.

Jofuku sailed for the land of Horaizan, but he never returned to the waiting Emperor; but ever since that time Mount Fuji has been said to be the fabled Horaizan and the home of hermits who had the secret of the elixir, and Jofuku has been worshiped as their patron god.

Now Sentaro determined to set out to find the hermits, and if he could, to become one, so that he might obtain the water of perpetual life. He remembered that as a child he had been told that not only did these hermits live on Mount Fuji, but that they were said to inhabit all the very high peaks.

So he left his old home to the care of his relatives, and started out on his quest. He traveled through all the mountainous regions of the land, climbing to the tops of the highest peaks, but never a hermit did he find.

At last, after wandering in an unknown region for many days, he met a hunter.

"Can you tell me," asked Sentaro, "where the hermits live who have the Elixir of Life?"

"No," said the hunter; "I can't tell you where such hermits live, but there is a notorious robber living in these parts. It is said that he is chief of a band of two hundred followers."

This odd answer irritated Sentaro very much, and he thought how foolish it was to waste more time in looking for the hermits in this way, so he decided to go at once to the shrine of Jofuku, who is worshiped as the patron god of the hermits in the south of Japan.

Sentaro reached the shrine and prayed for seven days, entreating Jofuku to show him the way to a hermit who could give him what he wanted so much to find.

At midnight of the seventh day, as Sentaro knelt in the temple, the door of the innermost shrine flew open, and Jofuku appeared in a luminous cloud, and calling to Sentaro to come nearer, spoke thus:

"Your desire is a very selfish one and cannot be easily granted. You think that you would like to become a hermit so as to find the Elixir of Life. Do you know how hard a hermit's life is? A hermit is only allowed to eat fruit and berries and the bark of pine trees; a hermit must cut himself off from the world so that his heart may become as pure as gold and free from every earthly desire. Gradually after following these strict rules, the hermit ceases to feel hunger or cold or heat, and his body becomes so light that he can ride on a crane or a carp, and can walk on water without getting his feet wet."

"You, Sentaro, are fond of good living and of every comfort. You are not even like an ordinary man, for you are exceptionally idle, and more sensitive to heat and cold than most people. You would never be able to go barefoot or to wear only one thin dress in the winter time! Do you think that you would ever have the patience or the endurance to live a hermit's life?"

"In answer to your prayer, however, I will help you in another way. I will send you to the country of Perpetual Life, where death never comes—where the people live forever!"

Saying this, Jofuku put into Sentaro's hand a little crane made of paper, telling him to sit on its back and it would carry him there.

Sentaro obeyed wonderingly. The crane grew large enough for him to ride on it with comfort. It then spread its wings, rose high in the air, and flew away over the mountains right out to sea.

Sentaro was at first quite frightened; but by degrees he grew accustomed to the swift flight through the air. On and on they went for thousands of miles. The bird never stopped for rest or food, but as it was a paper bird it doubtless did not require any nourishment, and strange to say, neither did Sentaro.

After several days they reached an island. The crane flew some distance inland and then alighted.

As soon as Sentaro got down from the bird's back, the crane folded up of its own accord and flew into his pocket.

Now Sentaro began to look about him wonderingly, curious to see what the country of Perpetual Life was like. He walked first round about the country and then through the town. Everything was, of course, quite strange, and different from his own land. But both the land and the people seemed prosperous, so he decided that it would be good for him to stay there and took up lodgings at one of the hotels.

The proprietor was a kind man, and when Sentaro told him that he was a stranger and had come to live there, he promised to arrange everything that was necessary with the governor of the city concerning Sentaro's sojourn there. He even found a house for his guest, and in this way Sentaro obtained his great wish and became a resident in the country of Perpetual Life.

Within the memory of all the islanders no man had ever died there, and sickness was a thing unknown. Priests had come over from India and China and told them of a beautiful country called Paradise, where happiness and bliss and contentment fill all men's hearts, but its gates could only be reached by dying. This tradition was handed down for ages from generation to generation—but none knew exactly what death was except that it led to Paradise.

Quite unlike Sentaro and other ordinary people, instead of having a great dread of death, they all, both rich and poor, longed for it as something good and desirable. They were all tired of their long, long lives, and longed to go to the happy land of contentment called Paradise of which the priests had told them centuries ago.

All this Sentaro soon found out by talking to the islanders. He found himself, according to his ideas, in the land of Topsyturvydom. Everything was upside down. He had wished to escape from dying. He had come to the land of Perpetual Life with great relief and joy, only to find that the inhabitants themselves, doomed never to die, would consider it bliss to find death.

What he had hitherto considered poison these people ate as good food, and all the things to which he had been accustomed as food they rejected. Whenever any merchants from other countries arrived, the rich people rushed to them eager to buy poisons. These they swallowed eagerly, hoping for death to come so that they might go to Paradise.

But what were deadly poisons in other lands were without effect in this strange place, and people who swallowed them with the hope of dying, only found that in a short time they felt better in health instead of worse.

Vainly they tried to imagine what death could be like. The wealthy would have given all their money and all their goods if they could but shorten their lives to two or three hundred years even. Without any change to live on forever seemed to this people wearisome and sad.

In the chemist shops there was a drug which was in constant demand, because after using it for a hundred years, it was supposed to turn the hair slightly gray and to bring about disorders of the stomach.

Sentaro was astonished to find that the poisonous globe fish was served up in restaurants as a delectable dish, and hawkers in the streets went about selling sauces made of Spanish flies. He never saw any one ill after eating these horrible things, nor did he ever see any one with as much as a cold.

Sentaro was delighted. He said to himself that he would never grow tired of living, and that he considered it profane to wish for death. He was the only happy man on the island. For his part he wished to live thousands of years and to enjoy life. He set himself up in business, and for the present never even dreamed of going back to his native land.

As years went by, however, things did not go as smoothly as at first. He had heavy losses in business, and several times some affairs went wrong with his neighbors. This caused him great annoyance.

Time passed like the flight of an arrow for him, for he was busy from morning till night. Three hundred years went by in this monotonous way, and then at last he began to grow tired of life in this country, and he longed to see his own land and his old home. However long he lived here, life would always be the same, so was it not foolish and wearisome to stay on here forever?

Sentaro, in his wish to escape from the country of Perpetual Life, recollected Jofuku, who had helped him before when he was wishing to escape from death—and he prayed to the saint to bring him back to his own land again.

No sooner did he pray than the paper crane popped out of his pocket. Sentaro was amazed to see that it had remained undamaged after all these years. Once more the bird grew and grew till it was large enough for him to mount it. As he did so, the bird spread its wings and flew, swiftly out across the sea in the direction of Japan.

Such was the willfulness of the man's nature that he looked back and regretted all he had left behind. He tried to stop the bird in vain. The crane held on its way for thousands of miles across the ocean.

Then a storm came on, and the wonderful paper crane got damp, crumpled up, and fell into the sea. Sentaro fell with it. Very much frightened at the thought of being drowned, he cried out loudly to Jofuku to save him. He looked round, but there was no ship in sight. He swallowed a quantity of seawater, which only increased his miserable plight. While he was thus struggling to keep himself afloat, he saw a monstrous shark swimming towards him. As it came nearer it opened its huge mouth ready to devour him. Sentaro was all but paralyzed with fear now that he felt his end so near, and screamed out as loudly as ever he could to Jofuku to come and rescue him.

Lo, and behold, Sentaro was awakened by his own screams, to find that during his long prayer he had fallen asleep before the shrine, and that all his extraordinary and frightful adventures had been only a wild dream. He was in a cold perspiration with fright, and utterly bewildered.

Suddenly a bright light came towards him, and in the light stood a messenger. The messenger held a book in his hand, and spoke to Sentaro:

"I am sent to you by Jofuku, who in answer to your prayer, has permitted you in a dream to see the land of Perpetual Life. But you grew weary of living there, and begged to be allowed to return to your native land so that you might die. Jofuku, so that he might try you, allowed you to drop into the sea, and then sent a shark to swallow you up. Your desire for death was not real, for even at that moment you cried out loudly and shouted for help."

"It is also vain for you to wish to become a hermit, or to find the Elixir of Life. These things are not for such as you—your life is not austere enough. It is best for you to go back to your paternal home, and to live a good and industrious life. Never neglect to keep the anniversaries of your ancestors, and make it your duty to provide for your children's future. Thus will you live to a good old age and be happy, but give up the vain desire to escape death, for no man can do that, and by this time you have surely found out that even when selfish desires are granted they do not bring happiness."

"In this book I give you there are many precepts good for you to know—if you study them, you will be guided in the way I have pointed out to you."

The angel disappeared as soon as he had finished speaking, and Sentaro took the lesson to heart. With the book in his hand he returned to his old home, and giving up all his old vain wishes, tried to live a good and useful life and to observe the lessons taught him in the book, and he and his house prospered henceforth.

The Spirit
of the Lantern

Some three hundred years ago, in the province of Kai and the town of Aoyagi, there lived a man named Koharu Tomosaburo, of well-known ancestry. His grandfather had been a retainer of Ota Dokan, the founder of Edo, and had committed suicide when his lord fell in battle.

This brave clansman's grandson was Tomosaburo, who, when this story begins, had been happily married for many years to a woman of the same province and was the proud father of a son some ten years of age.

At this time it happened, one day, that his wife fell suddenly ill and was unable to leave her bed. Physicians were called in but had to acknowledge themselves baffled by the curious symptoms of the patient: to relieve the paroxysms of pain from which she suffered, Moxa was applied and burned in certain spots down her back. But half a month passed by and the anxious household realized that there was no change for the better in the mysterious malady that was consuming her: day by day she seemed to lose ground and waste away.

Tomosaburo was a kind husband and scarcely left her bedside: day and night he tenderly ministered to his stricken wife, and did all in his power to alleviate her condition.

One evening, as he was sitting thus, worn out with the strain of nursing and anxiety, he fell into a doze. Suddenly there came a change in the light of the standing lantern, it flushed a brilliant red, then flared up into the air to the height of at least three feet, and within the crimson pillar of flame there appeared the figure of a woman.

Tomosaburo gazed in astonishment at the apparition, who thus addressed him:

"Your anxiety concerning your wife's illness is well known to me, therefore I have come to give you some good advice. The affliction with which she is visited is the punishment for some faults in her character. For this reason she is possessed of a devil. If you will worship me as a god, I will cast out the tormenting demon."

Now Tomosaburo was a brave, strong-minded samurai, to whom the sensation of fear was totally unknown.

He glared fiercely at the apparition, and then, half unconsciously, turned for the samurai's only safeguard, his sword, and drew it from its sheath. The sword is regarded as sacred by the Japanese knight and was supposed to possess the occult power assigned to the sign of the cross in medieval Europe— that of exorcising evil.

The spirit laughed superciliously when she saw his action.

"No motive but the kindest of intentions brought me here to proffer you my assistance in your trouble, but without the least appreciation of my goodwill you show this enmity towards me. However, your wife's life shall pay the penalty," and with these malicious words the phantom disappeared.

From that hour the unhappy woman's sufferings increased, and to the distress of all about her, she seemed about to draw her last breath.

Her husband was beside himself with grief. He realized at once what a false move he had made in driving away the friendly spirit in such an uncouth and hostile manner, and, now thoroughly alarmed at his wife's desperate plight, he was willing to comply with any demand, however strange. He thereupon prostrated himself before the family shrine and addressed fervent prayers to the Spirit of the Lantern, humbly imploring her pardon for his thoughtless and discourteous behavior.

From that very hour the invalid began to mend, and steadily improving day by day, her normal health was soon entirely regained, until it seemed to her as though her long and strange illness had been but an evil dream.

One evening after her recovery, when the husband and wife were sitting together and speaking joyfully of her unexpected and almost miraculous restoration to health, the lantern flared up as before and in the column of brilliant light the form of the spirit again appeared.

"Notwithstanding your unkind reception of me the last time I came, I have driven out the devil and saved your wife's life. In return for this service I have come to ask a favor of you, Tomosaburo San," said the spirit. "I have a daughter who is now of a marriageable age. The reason of my visit is to request you to find a suitable husband for her."

"But I am a human being," remonstrated the perplexed man, "and you are a spirit! We belong to different worlds, and a wide and impassable gulf separates us. How would it be possible for me to do as you wish?"

"It is an easier matter than you imagine," replied the spirit. "All you have to do is to take some blocks of *kiri* [*Paulownia imperialis*] wood [*Paulownia imperialis*] and to carve out from them several little figures of men; when they are finished I will bestow upon one of them the hand of my daughter."

"If that is all, then it is not so difficult as I thought, and I will undertake to do as you wish," assented Tomosaburo, and no sooner had the spirit vanished than he opened his tool box and set to work upon the appointed task with such alacrity that in a few days he had fashioned out in miniature several very creditable effigies of the desired bridegroom, and when the wooden dolls were completed he laid them out in a row upon his desk.

The next morning, on awaking, he lost no time in ascertaining what had befallen the quaint little figures, but apparently they had found favor with the spirit, for all had disappeared during the night. He now hoped that the strange and supernatural visitant would trouble them no more, but the next night she again appeared:

"Owing to your kind assistance my daughter's future is settled. As a mark of our gratitude for the trouble you have taken, we earnestly desire the presence of both yourself and your wife at the marriage feast. When the time arrives promise to come without fail."

By this time Tomosaburo was thoroughly wearied of these ghostly visitations and considered it highly obnoxious to be in league with such weird and intangible beings, yet fully aware of their powers of working evil, he dared not offend them. He racked his brains for some way of escape from this uncanny invitation, but before he could frame any reply suitable to the emergency, and while he was hesitating, the spirit vanished.

Long did the perplexed man ponder over the strange situation, but the more he thought the more embarrassed he became: and there seemed no solution of his dilemma.

The next night the spirit again returned.

"As I had the honour to inform you, we have prepared an entertainment at which your presence is desired. All is now in readiness. The wedding ceremony has taken place and the assembled company await your arrival with impatience. Kindly follow me at once!" and the wraith made imperious gestures to Tomosaburo and his wife to accompany her. With a sudden movement she darted from the lantern flame and glided out of the room, now and again looking back with furtive glances to see that they were surely following—and thus they passed, the spirit guiding them, along the passage to the outer porch.

The idea of accepting the spirit's hospitality was highly repugnant to the astonished couple, but remembering the dire consequences of his first refusal to comply with the ghostly visitor's request, Tomosaburo thought it wiser to simulate acquiescence. He was well aware that in some strange and incomprehensible manner his wife owed her sudden recovery to the spirit's agency, and for this boon he felt it would be both unseemly and ungrateful—and possibly dangerous—to refuse. In great embarrassment, and at a loss for any plausible excuse, he felt half dazed, and as though all capacity for voluntary action was deserting him.

What was Tomosaburo's surprise on reaching the entrance to find stationed there a procession, like the train of some great personage, awaiting him. On their appearance the liveried bearers hastened to bring forward two magnificent palanquins of lacquer and gold, and at the same moment a tall man garbed in ceremonial robes advanced and with a deep obeisance requested them not to hesitate, saying:

"Honored sir, these *kago*[1] are for your august conveyance—deign to enter so that we may proceed to your destination."

At the same time the members of the procession and the bearers bowed low, and in curious high-pitched voices all repeated the invitation in a chorus:

"Please deign to enter the *kago!*"

Both Tomosaburo and his wife were not only amazed at the splendor of the escort which had been provided for them, but they realized that what was happening to them was most mysterious, and might have unexpected consequences. However, it was too late to draw back now, and all they could do was to fall in with the arrangement with as bold a front as they could muster. They both stepped valiantly into the elaborately decorated *kago*; thereupon the attendants surrounded the palanquins, the bearers raised the shafts shoulder high, and the procession formed in line and set out on its ghostly expedition.

The night was still and very dark. Thick masses of sable cloud obscured the heavens, with no friendly gleams of moon or stars to illumine their unknown path, and peering through the bamboo blinds nothing met Tomosaburo's anxious gaze but the impenetrable gloom of the inky sky.

Seated in the palanquins the adventurous couple were undergoing a strange experience. To their mystified senses it did not seem as if the *kago* was being borne along over the ground in the ordinary manner, but the sensation was as though they were being swiftly impelled by some mysterious unseen force, which caused them to skim through the air like the flight of birds. After some time had elapsed the somber blackness of the night somewhat lifted, and they were dimly able to discern the curved outlines of a large mansion which they were now approaching, and which appeared to be situated in a spacious and thickly wooded park.

The bearers entered the large roofed gate and, crossing an intervening space of garden, carefully lowered their burdens before the main entrance of the house, where a body of servants and retainers were already waiting to welcome the expected guests with assiduous attentions. Tomosaburo and his wife alighted from their conveyances and were ushered into a reception room of great size and splendor, where, as soon as they were seated in the place of honor near the alcove, refreshments were served by a bevy of fair waiting maids in ceremonial costumes. As soon as they were rested from the fatigues of their journey an usher appeared and bowing profoundly to the bewildered newcomers announced that the marriage feast was about to be celebrated and their presence was requested without delay.

Following this guide they proceeded through the various anterooms and along the corridors. The whole interior of the mansion, the sumptuousness of its appointments and the delicate beauty of its finishings, were such as to fill their hearts with wonder and admiration.

The floors of the passages shone like mirrors, so fine was the quality of the satiny woods, and the richly inlaid ceilings showed that no expense or trouble had been spared in the selection of all that was ancient and rare, both in materials and workmanship. Certain of the pillars were formed by the trunks of petrified trees, brought from great distances, and on every side perfect taste and limitless wealth were apparent in every detail of the scheme of decoration.

More and more deeply impressed with his surroundings, Tomosaburo obediently followed in the wake of the ushers. As they neared the stately guest chamber an eerie and numbing sensation seemed to creep through his veins.

Observing more closely the surrounding figures that flitted to and fro, with a shock of horror he suddenly became aware that their faces were well known to him and of many in that shadowy throng he recognized the features and forms of friends and relatives long since dead. Along the corridors leading to the principal hall numerous attendants were gathered: all their features were familiar to Tomosaburo, but none of them betrayed the slightest sign of recognition. Gradually his dazed brain began to understand that he was visiting in the underworld, that everything about him was unreal—in fact, a dream of the past—and he feebly wondered of what hallucination he could be the victim to be thus abruptly bidden to such an illusory carnival, where all the wedding guests seemed to be denizens of the Meido, that dusky kingdom of departed spirits! But no time was left him for conjecture, for on reaching the anteroom they were immediately ushered into a magnificent hall where all preparations for the feast had been set out, and where the Elysian Strand[2] and the symbols of marriage were all duly arranged according to time-honored custom.

Here the bridegroom and his bride were seated in state, both attired in elegant robes as befitting the occasion. Tomosaburo, who had acted such a strange and important part in providing the farcical groom for this unheard-of marriage, gazed searchingly at the newly wedded husband, whose mien was quite dignified and imposing, and whose thick dark locks were crowned with a nobleman's coronet. He wondered what part the wooden figures he had carved according to the spirit's behest had taken in the composition of the bridegroom he now saw before him. Strangely, indeed, his features bore a striking resemblance to the little puppets that Tomosaburo had fashioned from the *kiri* wood some days before.

The nuptial couple were receiving the congratulations of the assembled guests, and no sooner had Tomosaburo and his wife entered the room than the wedding party all came forward in a body to greet them and to offer thanks for their condescension in gracing that happy occasion with their presence. They were ceremoniously conducted to seats in a place of honor, and invited with great cordiality to participate in the evening's entertainment.

Servants then entered bearing all sorts of tempting dainties piled on lacquer trays in the form of large shells; the feast was spread before the whole assemblage; wine flowed in abundance, and by degrees conversation, laughter, and merriment became universal and the banquet hall echoed with the carousal of the ghostly throng.

Under the influence of the good cheer Tomosaburo's apprehension and alarm of his weird environment gradually wore off, he partook freely of the refreshments, and associated himself more and more with the gaiety and joviality of the evening's revel.

The night wore on and when the hour of midnight struck the banquet was at its height.

In the mirth and glamour of that strange marriage feast Tomosaburo had lost all track of time, when suddenly the clear sound of a cock's crow penetrated his clouded brain and, looking up, the transparency of the shoji[3] of the room began to slowly whiten in the gray of dawn. Like a flash of lightning Tomosaburo and his wife found themselves transported back, safe and sound, into their own room.

On reflection he found his better nature more and more troubled by such an uncanny experience, and he spent much time pondering over the matter, which seemed to require such delicate handling. He determined that at all costs communications must be broken off with the importunate spirit.

A few days passed and Tomosaburo began to cherish the hope that he had seen the last of the Spirit of the Lantern, but his congratulations on escaping her unwelcome attentions proved premature. That very night, no sooner had he laid himself down to rest, than lo! and behold, the lantern shot up in the familiar shaft of light, and there in the lurid glow appeared the spirit, looking more than ever bent on mischief. Tomosaburo lost all patience. Glaring savagely at the unwelcome visitant he seized his wooden pillow[4] and, determining to rid himself of her persecutions once and for all, he exerted his whole strength and hurled it straight at the intruder. His aim was true, and the missile struck the goblin squarely on the forehead, overturning the lantern and plunging the room into black darkness. "Wa, Wa!" wailed the spirit in a thin haunting cry, that gradually grew fainter and fainter till she finally disappeared like a luminous trail of vanishing blue smoke.

From that very hour Tomosaburo's wife was again stricken with her former malady, and no remedies being of any avail, within two days it took a turn for the worse and she died.

The sorrow-stricken husband bitterly regretted his impetuous action in giving way to that fatal fit of anger and, moreover, in appearing so forgetful of the past favor he had received from the spirit. He therefore prayed earnestly to the offended apparition, apologizing with humble contrition for his cruelty and ingratitude.

But the Spirit of the Lantern had been too deeply outraged to return, and Tomosaburo's repentance for his rash impulse proved all in vain.

These melancholy events caused the unhappy husband to take a strong aversion to the house, which he felt sure must be haunted, and he decided to leave that neighborhood with as little delay as possible.

As soon as a suitable dwelling was found and the details of his migration arranged, the carriers were summoned to transport his household goods to the new abode, but to the alarm and consternation of everyone, when the servants attempted to move the furniture, the whole contents of the house by some unseen power adhered fast to the floor, and no human power was available to dislodge them.

Then Tomosaburo's little son fell ill and died. Such was the revenge of the Spirit of the Lantern.

Notes

1. A *kago* in this context is a palanquin.
2. *Horai Dai*, the Eastern fairyland, where death and sickness never come, and where the fabulous old couple of Takasayo, paragons of conjugal felicity and constancy, live forever in the shade of the evergreen pines, while storks and green-tailed tortoises, emblems of prosperity and ten thousand years of life, keep them company.
3. Shoji are the sliding screens which takes the place of doors and windows in a Japanese house—the framework is of a fine latticework of wood, covered with white paper sufficiently transparent to let in the light.
4. The old Japanese pillow was a wooden stand, on the top of which was a groove; in this was placed a small roll of cotton wool covered with silk or crepe, etc.

The Serpent with Eight Heads

Did you ever hear the story of the Eight-Headed Serpent? If not, I will tell it to you. It is rather a long one, and we must go a good way back to get to the beginning of it. In fact, we must go back to the beginning of the world.

After the world had been created, it became the property of a very powerful fairy; and when this fairy was about to die, he divided it between his two boys and his girl.

The girl, called Ama, was given the sun; the eldest boy, called Susano, was given the sea; and the second boy, whose name I forget, was given the moon. Well, the Moon Boy behaved himself properly; and you can still see his jolly round face on a clear night when the moon is full. But Susano was very angry and disappointed at having nothing but the cold wet sea to live in. So up he rushed into the sky, burst into the beautiful room inside the sun, where his sister was sitting with her maidens weaving gold and silver dresses, broke their spindles, trampled upon their work, and in short did all the mischief he could, and frightened the poor maids to death. As for Ama, she ran away as fast as she could, and hid herself in a cave on the side of a mountain full of rocks and crags. When she had got into the cave and had shut the door, the whole world became pitch dark. For she was the fairy who ruled the sun, and could make it shine or not as she chose. In fact, some people say that the light of the sun is really nothing else than the brightness of her own bright eyes. Anyhow, there was great trouble over her disappearance. What was to be done to make the world light again? All sorts of plans were tried. At last, knowing that she was curious and always liked to see everything that was going on, the other fairies got up a dance outside the door of the cave.

When Ama heard the noise of the dancing and singing and laughing, she could not help opening the door a tiny bit, in order to peep through the chink at the fun the other fairies were having. This was just what they had been watching for. "Look here!" cried they. "Look at this new fairy more beautiful than yourself!" and therewith they thrust forward a mirror. Ama did not know that the face in the mirror was only a reflection of her own; and, more and more curious to know who the new fairy could be, she ventured outside the door, where she was caught hold of by the other fairies, who piled up the entrance of the cave with big rocks, so that no one could ever go into it again. Seeing that she had been tricked into coming out of the cave, and that there was no use in sulking any longer, Ama agreed to go back to the sun and shine upon the world as before, provided her brother were punished and sent away in disgrace; for really he was not safe to live with. This was done. Susa was beaten to within an inch of his life, and expelled from the society of the other fairies, with orders never to show himself again.

So poor Susa, having been turned out of fairyland, was obliged to come down to the earth. While walking one day on the bank of a river, he happened to see an old man and an old woman with their arms round their young daughter, and crying bitterly. "What is the matter?" asked Susa. "Oh!" said they, their voice choked with sobs, "we used to have eight daughters. But in a marsh near our hut there lives a huge Eight-Headed Serpent, who comes out once every year, and eats up one of them. We have now only one daughter left, and today is the day when the Serpent will come to eat her, and then we shall have none. Please, good Sir, can you not do something to help us?"

"Of course," answered Susa; "it will be quite easy. Do not be sad any longer. I am a fairy, and I will save your daughter." So he told them to brew some beer, and showed them how to make a fence with eight gates in it, and a wooden stand inside each gate, and a large vat of beer on each stand. This they did; and just as all had been arranged in the way Susa had bidden them, the Serpent came. So huge was he, that his body trained over eight hills and eight valleys as he wriggled along. But as he had eight heads, he also had eight noses, which made him able to smell eight times as quickly as any other creature. So, smelling the beer from afar off he at once glided towards it, went inside the fence, dipped one of his heads into each of the eight vats, and drank and drank and drank, till he got quite tipsy. Then all his heads dropped down fast asleep; and Susa, jumping up from the hole where he had lain hidden, drew his sword, and cut them all off. He cut the body to pieces too. But, strange to say, when cutting the tail, the blade of his sword snapped. It had struck against something hard. As the Serpent was now dead, there was no danger in going up to it, and finding out what the hard thing was. It turned out to be itself a sword all set with precious stones — the most beautiful sword you ever saw. Susa took the sword, and married the beautiful young girl; and he was very kind to her, although he had been so rude to his elder sister. They spent the rest of their lives in a beautiful palace, which was built on purpose for them; and the old father and mother lived there too. When the old father and mother, and Susa and his wife had all died, the sword was handed down to their children, and grandchildren; and it now belongs to the Emperor of Japan, who looks upon it as one of his most precious treasures.

A Passional Karma

There once lived in the district of Ushigome, in Edo, a *hatamoto*[1] called Iijima Heizayemon, whose only daughter, Tsuyu, was beautiful as her name, which signifies "Morning Dew." Iijima took a second wife when his daughter was about sixteen; and, finding that O-Tsuyu could not be happy with her stepmother, he had a pretty villa built for the girl at Yanagijima, as a separate residence, and gave her an excellent maidservant, called O-Yone, to wait upon her.

O-Tsuyu lived happily enough in her new home until one day when the family physician, Yamamoto Shijo, paid her a visit in company with a young samurai named Hagiwara Shinzaburo, who resided in the Nedzu quarter. Shinzaburo was an unusually handsome lad, and very gentle; and the two young people fell in love with each other at sight. Even before the brief visit was over, they contrived—unheard by the old doctor—to pledge themselves to each other for life. And, at parting, O-Tsuyu whispered to the youth, *"Remember! If you do not come to see me again, I shall certainly die!"*

Shinzaburo never forgot those words; and he was only too eager to see more of O-Tsuyu. But etiquette forbade him to make the visit alone: he was obliged to wait for some other chance to accompany the doctor, who had promised to take him to the villa a second time. Unfortunately the old man did not keep this promise. He had perceived the sudden affection of O-Tsuyu; and he feared that her father would hold him responsible for any serious results. Iijima Heizayemon had a reputation for cutting off heads. And the more Shijo thought about the possible consequences of his introduction of Shinzaburo at the Iijima villa, the more he became afraid. Therefore he purposely abstained from calling upon his young friend.

Months passed; and O-Tsuyu, little imagining the true cause of Shinzaburo's neglect, believed that her love had been scorned. Then she pined away, and died. Soon afterwards, the faithful servant O-Yone also died, through grief at the loss of her mistress; and the two were buried side by side in the cemetery of Shin-Banzui-In, a temple which still stands in the neighborhood of Dan-go-Zaka, where the famous chrysanthemum shows are yearly held.

II

Shinzaburo knew nothing of what had happened; but his disappointment and his anxiety had resulted in a prolonged illness. He was slowly recovering, but still very weak, when he unexpectedly received another visit from Yamamoto Shijo. The old man made a number of plausible excuses for his apparent neglect. Shinzaburo said to him: "I have been sick ever since the beginning of spring; even now I cannot eat anything... Was it not rather unkind of you never to call? I thought that we were to make another visit together to the house of the Lady Iijima; and I wanted to take to her some little present as a return for our kind reception. Of course I could not go by myself."

Shijo gravely responded, "I am very sorry to tell you that the young lady is dead!"

"Dead!" repeated Shinzaburo, turning white, "Did you say that she is dead?"

The doctor remained silent for a moment, as if collecting himself; then he resumed, in the quick light tone of a man resolved not to take trouble seriously:

"My great mistake was in having introduced you to her; for it seems that she fell in love with you at once. I am afraid that you must have said something to encourage this affection—when you were in that little room together. At all events, I saw how she felt towards you; and then I became uneasy, fearing that her father might come to hear of the matter, and lay the whole blame upon me. So—to be quite frank with you—I decided that it would be better not to call upon you; and I purposely stayed away for a long time. But, only a few days ago, happening to visit Iijima's house, I heard, to my great surprise, that his daughter had died, and that her servant O-Yone had also died. Then, remembering all that had taken place, I knew that the young lady must have died of love for you... [*Laughing*] Ah, you are really a sinful fellow! Yes, you are! [*Laughing*] Isn't it a sin to have been born so handsome that the girls die for love of you?[2] [*Seriously*] Well, we must leave the dead to the dead. It is no use to talk further about the matter; all that you now can do for her is to repeat the Nembutsu[3].... Goodbye."

And the old man retired hastily, anxious to avoid further converse about the painful event for which he felt himself to have been unwittingly responsible.

III

Shinzaburo long remained stupefied with grief by the news of O-Tsuyu's death. But as soon as he found himself again able to think clearly, he inscribed the dead girl's name upon a mortuary tablet, and placed the tablet in the Buddhist shrine of his house, and set offerings before it, and recited prayers. Every day thereafter he presented offerings, and repeated the Nembutsu; and the memory of O-Tsuyu was never absent from his thought.

Nothing occurred to change the monotony of his solitude before the time of the Bon—the great Festival of the Dead—which begins upon the thirteenth day of the seventh month. Then he decorated his house, and prepared everything for the festival; hanging out the lanterns that guide the returning spirits, and setting the food of ghosts on the *shoryodana*, or Shelf of Souls. And on the first evening of the Bon, after sundown, he kindled a small lamp before the tablet of O-Tsuyu, and lighted the lanterns.

The night was clear, with a great moon, and windless, and very warm. Shinzaburo sought the coolness of his veranda. Clad only in a light summer robe, he sat there thinking, dreaming, sorrowing; sometimes fanning himself;

sometimes making a little smoke to drive the mosquitoes away. Everything was quiet. It was a lonesome neighborhood, and there were few passersby. He could hear only the soft rushing of a neighboring stream, and the shrilling of night insects.

But all at once this stillness was broken by a sound of women's geta[4] approaching—*kara-kon, kara-kon*—and the sound drew nearer and nearer, quickly, till it reached the live hedge surrounding the garden. Then Shinzaburo, feeling curious, stood on tiptoe, so as to look over the hedge; and he saw two women passing. One, who was carrying a beautiful lantern decorated with peony flowers,[5] appeared to be a servant; the other was a slender girl of about seventeen, wearing a long-sleeved robe embroidered with designs of autumn blossoms. Almost at the same instant both women turned their faces toward Shinzaburo—and to his utter astonishment, he recognized O-Tsuyu and her servant O-Yone.

They stopped immediately; and the girl cried out, "Oh, how strange!... Hagiwara Sama!"

Shinzaburo simultaneously called to the maid: "O-Yone! Ah, you are O-Yone! I remember you very well."

"Hagiwara Sama!" exclaimed O-Yone in a tone of supreme amazement. "Never could I have believed it possible!... Sir, we were told that you had died."

"How extraordinary!" cried Shinzaburo. "Why, I was told that both of you were dead!"

"Ah, what a hateful story!" returned O-Yone. "Why repeat such unlucky words?... Who told you?"

"Please to come in," said Shinzaburo, "here we can talk better. The garden gate is open."

So they entered, and exchanged greeting; and when Shinzaburo had made them comfortable, he said:

"I trust that you will pardon my discourtesy in not having called upon you for so long a time. But Shijo, the doctor, about a month ago, told me that you had both died."

"So it was he who told you?" exclaimed O-Yone. "It was very wicked of him to say such a thing. Well, it was also Shijo who told us that *you* were dead. I think that he wanted to deceive you,which was not a difficult thing to do, because you are so confiding and trustful. Possibly my mistress betrayed her liking for you in some words which found their way to her father's ears; and, in that case, O-Kuni—the new wife—might have planned to make the doctor tell you that we were dead, so as to bring about a separation. Anyhow, when my mistress heard that you had died, she wanted to cut off her hair immediately, and to become a nun. But I was able to prevent her from cutting off her hair; and I persuaded her at last to become a nun only in her heart. Afterwards her father wished her to marry a certain young man; and she refused. Then there was a great deal of trouble, chiefly caused by O-Kuni; and we went away from the villa, and found a very small house in Yanaka-no-Sasaki. There we are now just barely able to live, by doing a little private work…. My mistress has been constantly repeating the Nembutsu for your sake. Today, being the first day of the Bon, we went to visit the temples; and we were on our way home—thus late—when this strange meeting happened."

"Oh, how extraordinary!" cried Shinzaburo. "Can it be true? Or is it only a dream? Here I, too, have been constantly reciting the Nembutsu before a tablet with her name upon it! Look!" And he showed them O-Tsuyu's tablet in its place upon the Shelf of Souls.

"We are more than grateful for your kind remembrance," returned O-Yone, smiling…. "Now as for my mistress," she continued, turning towards O-Tsuyu, who had all the while remained demure and silent, half hiding her face with her sleeve, "as for my mistress, she actually says that she would not mind being disowned by her father for the time of seven existences,[6] or even being killed by him, for your sake! Come! will you not allow her to stay here tonight?"

Shinzaburo turned pale for joy. He answered in a voice trembling with emotion:

"Please remain; but do not speak loud—because there is a troublesome fellow living close by, a *ninsomi*[7] called Hakuodo Yusai, who tells peoples fortunes by looking at their faces. He is inclined to be curious; and it is better that he should not know."

The two women remained that night in the house of the young samurai, and returned to their own home a little before daybreak. And after that night they came every night for seven nights, whether the weather were foul or fair, always at the same hour. And Shinzaburo became more and more attached to the girl; and the twain were fettered, each to each, by that bond of illusion which is stronger than bands of iron.

IV

Now there was a man called Tomozo, who lived in a small cottage adjoining Shinzaburo's residence. Tomozo and his wife O-Mine were both employed by Shinzaburo as servants. Both seemed to be devoted to their young master; and by his help they were able to live in comparative comfort.

One night, at a very late hour, Tomozo heard the voice of a woman in his master's apartment; and this made him uneasy. He feared that Shinzaburo, being very gentle and affectionate, might be made the dupe of some cunning wanton, in which event the domestics would be the first to suffer. He therefore resolved to watch; and on the following night he stole on tiptoe to Shinzaburo's dwelling, and looked through a chink in one of the sliding shutters. By the glow of a night lantern within the sleeping room, he was able to perceive that his master and a strange woman were talking together under the mosquito net. At first he could not see the woman distinctly. Her back was turned to him; he only observed that she was very slim, and that she appeared to be very young, judging from the fashion of her dress and hair.[8] Putting his ear to the chink, he could hear the conversation plainly. The woman said:

"And if I should be disowned by my father, would you then let me come and live with you?"

Shinzaburo answered:

"Most assuredly I would—nay, I should be glad of the chance. But there is no reason to fear that you will ever be disowned by your father; for you are his only daughter, and he loves you very much. What I do fear is that someday we shall be cruelly separated."

She responded softly:

"Never, never could I even think of accepting any other man for my husband. Even if our secret were to become known, and my father were to kill me for what I have done, still—after death itself—I could never cease to think of you. And I am now quite sure that you yourself would not be able to live very long without me." Then clinging closely to him, with her lips at his neck, she caressed him; and he returned her caresses.

Tomozo wondered as he listened, because the language of the woman was not the language of a common woman, but the language of a lady of rank.[9] Then he determined at all hazards to get one glimpse of her face; and he crept round the house, backwards and forwards, peering through every crack and chink. And at last he was able to see; but therewith an icy trembling seized him; and the hair of his head stood up.

For the face was the face of a woman long dead, and the fingers caressing were fingers of naked bone, and of the body below the waist there was not anything: it melted off into thinnest trailing shadow. Where the eyes of the lover deluded saw youth and grace and beauty, there appeared to the eyes of the watcher horror only, and the emptiness of death. Simultaneously another woman's figure, and a weirder, rose up from within the chamber, and swiftly made toward the watcher, as if discerning his presence. Then, in uttermost terror, he fled to the dwelling of Hakuodo Yusai, and, knocking frantically at the doors, succeeded in arousing him.

V

Hakuodo Yusai, the *ninsomi*, was a very old man; but in his time he had traveled much, and he had heard and seen so many things that he could not be easily surprised. Yet the story of the terrified Tomozo both alarmed and amazed him. He had read in ancient Chinese books of love between the living and the dead; but he had never believed it possible. Now, however, he felt convinced that the statement of Tomozo was not a falsehood, and that something very strange was really going on in the house of Hagiwara. Should the truth prove to be what Tomozo imagined, then the young samurai was a doomed man.

"If the woman be a ghost," said Yusai to the frightened servant, "—if the woman be a ghost, your master must die very soon, unless something extraordinary can be done to save him. And if the woman be a ghost, the signs of death will appear upon his face. For the spirit of the living is *yoki*, and pure; the spirit of the dead is *inki*, and unclean: the one is Positive, the other Negative. He whose bride is a ghost cannot live. Even though in his blood there existed the force of a life of one hundred years, that force must quickly perish…. Still, I shall do all that I can to save Hagiwara Sama. And in the meantime, Tomozo, say nothing to any other person, not even to your wife, about this matter. At sunrise I shall call upon your master."

VI

When questioned next morning by Yusai, Shinzaburo at first attempted to deny that any women had been visiting the house; but finding this artless policy of no avail, and perceiving that the old man's purpose was altogether unselfish, he was finally persuaded to acknowledge what had really occurred, and to give his reasons for wishing to keep the matter a secret. As for the lady Iijima, he intended, he said, to make her his wife as soon as possible.

"Oh, madness!" cried Yusai, losing all patience in the intensity of his alarm. "Know, sir, that the people who have been coming here, night after night, are dead! Some frightful delusion is upon you! Why, the simple fact that you long supposed O-Tsuyu to be dead, and repeated the Nembutsu for her, and made offerings before her tablet, is itself the proof! The lips of the dead have touched you! The hands of the dead have caressed you! Even at this moment I see in your face the signs of death—and you will not believe! Listen to me now, sir, I beg of you, if you wish to save yourself: otherwise you have less than twenty days to live. They told you—those people—that they were residing in the district of Shitaya, in Yanaka-no-Sasaki. Did you ever visit them at that place? No! Of course you did not! Then go today, as soon as you can, to Yanaka-no-Sasaki, and try to find their home!"

And having uttered this counsel with the most vehement earnestness, Hakuodo Yusai abruptly took his departure.

Shinzaburo, startled though not convinced, resolved after a moment's reflection to follow the advice of the *ninsomi*, and to go to Shitaya. It was yet early in the morning when he reached the quarter of Yanaka-no-Sasaki, and began his search for the dwelling of O-Tsuyu. He went through every street and side street, read all the names inscribed at the various entrances, and made inquiries whenever an opportunity presented itself. But he could not find anything resembling the little house mentioned by O-Yone; and none of the people whom he questioned knew of any house in the quarter inhabited by two single women. Feeling at last certain that further research would be useless, he turned homeward by the shortest way, which happened to lead through the grounds of the temple Shin-Banzui-In.

Suddenly his attention was attracted by two new tombs, placed side by side, at the rear of the temple. One was a common tomb, such as might have been erected for a person of humble rank: the other was a large and handsome monument; and hanging before it was a beautiful peony lantern, which had probably been left there at the time of the Festival of the Dead. Shinzaburo remembered that the peony lantern carried by O-Yone was exactly similar; and the coincidence impressed him as strange. He looked again at the tombs; but the tombs explained nothing. Neither bore any personal name—only the Buddhist *kaimyo*, or posthumous appellation. Then he determined to seek information at the temple. An acolyte stated, in reply to his questions, that the large tomb had been recently erected for the daughter of Iijima Heizayemon, the *hatamoto* of Ushigome; and that the small tomb next to it was that of her servant O-Yone, who had died of grief soon after the young lady's funeral.

Immediately to Shinzaburo's memory there recurred, with another and sinister meaning, the words of O-Yone: *"We went away, and found a very small house in Yanaka-no-Sasaki. There we are now just barely able to live—by doing a little private work…"* Here was indeed the very small house, and in Yanaka-no-Sasaki. But the little *private work…*?

Terror-stricken, the samurai hastened with all speed to the house of Yusai, and begged for his counsel and assistance. But Yusai declared himself unable to be of any aid in such a case. All that he could do was to send Shinzaburo to the high priest Ryoseki, of Shin-Banzui-In, with a letter praying for immediate religious help.

VII

The high priest Ryoseki was a learned and a holy man. By spiritual vision he was able to know the secret of any sorrow, and the nature of the karma that had caused it. He heard unmoved the story of Shinzaburo, and said to him:

"A very great danger now threatens you, because of an error committed in one of your former states of existence. The karma that binds you to the dead is very strong; but if I tried to explain its character, you would not be able to understand. I shall therefore tell you only this, that the dead person has no desire to injure you out of hate, feels no enmity towards you: she is influenced, on the contrary, by the most passionate affection for you. Probably the girl has been in love with you from a time long preceding your present life, from a time of not less than three or four past existences; and it would seem that, although necessarily changing her form and condition at each succeeding birth, she has not been able to cease from following after you. Therefore it will not be an easy thing to escape from her influence... But now I am going to lend you this powerful *mamori*.[10] It is a pure gold image of that Buddha called the Sea-Sounding Tathagata—*Kai-On-Nyorai*—because his preaching of the Law sounds through the world like the sound of the sea. And this little image is especially a *shiryo-yoke*,[11] which protects the living from the dead. This you must wear, in its covering, next to your body, under the girdle... Besides, I shall presently perform in the temple, a *segaki*-service[12] for the repose of the troubled spirit.... And here is a holy sutra, called *Ubo-Darani-Kyo*, or "Treasure-Raining Sutra"[13] you must be careful to recite it every night in your house—without fail... Furthermore I shall give you this package of *o-fuda*;[14] you must paste one of them over every opening of your house, no matter how small. If you do this, the power of the holy texts will prevent the dead from entering. But—whatever may happen—do not fail to recite the sutra."

Shinzaburo humbly thanked the high priest; and then, taking with him the image, the sutra, and the bundle of sacred texts, he made all haste to reach his home before the hour of sunset.

VIII

With Yusai's advice and help, Shinzaburo was able before dark to fix the holy texts over all the apertures of his dwelling. Then the *ninsomi* returned to his own house, leaving the youth alone.

Night came, warm and clear. Shinzaburo made fast the doors, bound the precious amulet about his waist, entered his mosquito net, and by the glow of a night lantern began to recite the *Ubo-Darani-Kyo*. For a long time he chanted the words, comprehending little of their meaning; then he tried to obtain some rest. But his mind was still too much disturbed by the strange events of the day. Midnight passed; and no sleep came to him. At last he heard the boom of the great temple bell of Dentsu-In announcing the eighth hour.[15]

It ceased; and Shinzaburo suddenly heard the sound of geta approaching from the old direction, but this time more slowly: *karan-koron, karan-koron!* At once a cold sweat broke over his forehead. Opening the sutra hastily, with trembling hand, he began again to recite it aloud. The steps came nearer and nearer—reached the living hedge—stopped! Then, strange to say, Shinzaburo felt unable to remain under his mosquito net: something stronger even than his fear impelled him to look; and, instead of continuing to recite the *Ubo-Darani-Kyo*, he foolishly approached the shutters, and through a chink peered out into the night. Before the house he saw O-Tsuyu standing, and O-Yone with the peony lantern; and both of them were gazing at the Buddhist texts pasted above the entrance. Never before—not even in what time she lived—had O-Tsuyu appeared so beautiful; and Shinzaburo felt his heart drawn towards her with a power almost resistless. But the terror of death and the terror of the unknown restrained; and there went on within him such a struggle between his love and his fear that he became as one suffering in the body the pains of the Shonetsu Hell.[16]

Presently he heard the voice of the maidservant, saying:

"My dear mistress, there is no way to enter. The heart of Hagiwara Sama must have changed. For the promise that he made last night has been broken; and the doors have been made fast to keep us out… We cannot go in tonight… It will be wiser for you to make up your mind not to think any more about him, because his feeling towards you has certainly changed. It is evident that he does not want to see you. So it will be better not to give yourself any more trouble for the sake of a man whose heart is so unkind."

But the girl answered, weeping:

"Oh, to think that this could happen after the pledges which we made to each other! Often I was told that the heart of a man changes as quickly as the sky of autumn; yet surely the heart of Hagiwara Sama cannot be so cruel that he should really intend to exclude me in this way! Dear Yone, please find some means of taking me to him… Unless you do, I will never, never go home again."

Thus she continued to plead, veiling her face with her long sleeves, and very beautiful she looked, and very touching; but the fear of death was strong upon her lover.

O-Yone at last made answer, "My dear young lady, why will you trouble your mind about a man who seems to be so cruel? Well, let us see if there be no way to enter at the back of the house: come with me!"

And taking O-Tsuyu by the hand, she led her away toward the rear of the dwelling; and there the two disappeared as suddenly as the light disappears when the flame of a lamp is blown out.

IX

Night after night the shadows came at the Hour of the Ox; and nightly Shinzaburo heard the weeping of O-Tsuyu. Yet he believed himself saved, little imagining that his doom had already been decided by the character of his dependents.

Tomozo had promised Yusai never to speak to any other person—not even to O-Mine—of the strange events that were taking place. But Tomozo was not long suffered by the haunters to rest in peace. Night after night O-Yone entered into his dwelling, and roused him from his sleep, and asked him to remove the *o-fuda* placed over one very small window at the back of his master's house. And Tomozo, out of fear, as often promised her to take away the *o-fuda* before the next sundown; but never by day could he make up his mind to remove it, believing that evil was intended to Shinzaburo. At last, in a night of storm, O-Yone startled him from slumber with a cry of reproach, and stooped above his pillow, and said to him: "Have a care how you trifle with us! If, by tomorrow night, you do not take away that text, you shall learn how I can hate!" And she made her face so frightful as she spoke that Tomozo nearly died of terror.

O-Mine, the wife of Tomozo, had never till then known of these visits: even to her husband they had seemed like bad dreams. But on this particular night it chanced that, waking suddenly, she heard the voice of a woman talking to Tomozo. Almost in the same moment the talking ceased; and when O-Mine looked about her, she saw, by the light of the night lamp, only her husband—shuddering and white with fear. The stranger was gone; the doors were fast: it seemed impossible that anybody could have entered. Nevertheless the jealousy of the wife had been aroused; and she began to chide and to question Tomozo in such a manner that he thought himself obliged to betray the secret, and to explain the terrible dilemma in which he had been placed.

Then the passion of O-Mine yielded to wonder and alarm; but she was a subtle woman, and she devised immediately a plan to save her husband by the sacrifice of her master. And she gave Tomozo a cunning counsel, telling him to make conditions with the dead.

They came again on the following night at the Hour of the Ox; and O-Mine hid herself on hearing the sound of their coming—*karan-koron, karan-koron!* But Tomozo went out to meet them in the dark, and even found courage to say to them what his wife had told him to say:

"It is true that I deserve your blame; but I had no wish to cause you anger. The reason that the *o-fuda* has not been taken away is that my wife and I are able to live only by the help of Hagiwara Sama, and that we cannot expose him to any danger without bringing misfortune upon ourselves. But if we could obtain the sum of a hundred *ryo* in gold, we should be able to please you, because we should then need no help from anybody. Therefore if you will give us a hundred *ryo*, I can take the *o-fuda* away without being afraid of losing our only means of support."

When he had uttered these words, O-Yone and O-Tsuyu looked at each other in silence for a moment. Then O-Yone said:

"Mistress, I told you that it was not right to trouble this man, as we have no just cause of ill will against him. But it is certainly useless to fret yourself about Hagiwara Sama, because his heart has changed towards you. Now once again, my dear young lady, let me beg you not to think any more about him!"

But O-Tsuyu, weeping, made answer:

"Dear Yone, whatever may happen, I cannot possibly keep myself from thinking about him! You know that you can get a hundred *ryo* to have the *o-fuda* taken off… Only once more, I pray, dear Yone! Only once more bring me face to face with Hagiwara Sama—I beseech you!" And hiding her face with her sleeve, she thus continued to plead.

"Oh! why will you ask me to do these things?" responded O-Yone. "You know very well that I have no money. But since you will persist in this whim of yours, in spite of all that I can say, I suppose that I must try to find the money somehow, and to bring it here tomorrow night…" Then, turning to the faithless Tomozo, she said: "Tomozo, I must tell you that Hagiwara Sama now wears upon his body a *mamori* called by the name of *Kai-On-Nyorai*, and that so long as he wears it we cannot approach him. So you will have to get that *mamori* away from him, by some means or other, as well as to remove the *o-fuda*."

Tomozo feebly made answer:

"That also I can do, if you will promise to bring me the hundred *ryo*."

"Well, mistress," said O-Yone, "you will wait, will you not, until tomorrow night?"

"Oh, dear Yone!" sobbed the other, "have we to go back tonight again without seeing Hagiwara Sama? Ah! It is cruel!"

And the shadow of the mistress, weeping, was led away by the shadow of the maid.

X

Another day went, and another night came, and the dead came with it. But this time no lamentation was heard without the house of Hagiwara; for the faithless servant found his reward at the Hour of the Ox, and removed the *o-fuda*. Moreover he had been able, while his master was at the bath, to steal from its case the golden *mamori*, and to substitute for it an image of copper; and he had buried the *Kai-On-Nyorai* in a desolate field. So the visitants found nothing to oppose their entering. Veiling their faces with their sleeves they rose and passed, like a streaming of vapor, into the little window from over which the holy text had been torn away. But what happened thereafter within the house Tomozo never knew.

The sun was high before he ventured again to approach his master's dwelling, and to knock upon the sliding doors. For the first time in years he obtained no response; and the silence made him afraid. Repeatedly he called, and received no answer. Then, aided by O-Mine, he succeeded in effecting an entrance and making his way alone to the sleeping-room, where he called again in vain. He rolled back the rumbling shutters to admit the light; but still within the house there was no stir. At last he dared to lift a corner of the mosquito net. But no sooner had he looked beneath than he fled from the house, with a cry of horror.

Shinzaburo was dead—hideously dead—and his face was the face of a man who had died in the uttermost agony of fear—and lying beside him in the bed were the bones of a woman! And the bones of the arms, and the bones of the hands, clung fast about his neck.

XI

Hakuodo Yusai, the fortune teller, went to view the corpse at the prayer of the faithless Tomozo. The old man was terrified and astonished at the spectacle, but looked about him with a keen eye. He soon perceived that the *o-fuda* had been taken from the little window at the back of the house; and on searching the body of Shinzaburo, he discovered that the golden *mamori* had been taken from its wrapping, and a copper image of Fudo put in place of it. He suspected Tomozo of the theft; but the whole occurrence was so very extraordinary that he thought it prudent to consult with the priest Ryoseki before taking further action. Therefore, after having made a careful examination of the premises, he betook himself to the temple Shin-Banzui-In, as quickly as his aged limbs could bear him.

Ryoseki, without waiting to hear the purpose of the old man's visit, at once invited him into a private apartment.

"You know that you are always welcome here," said Ryoseki. "Please seat yourself at ease... Well, I am sorry to tell you that Hagiwara Sama is dead."

Yusai wonderingly exclaimed: "Yes, he is dead; but how did you learn of it?"

The priest responded:

"Hagiwara Sama was suffering from the results of an evil karma; and his attendant was a bad man. What happened to Hagiwara Sama was unavoidable; his destiny had been determined from a time long before his last birth. It will be better for you not to let your mind be troubled by this event."

Yusai said:

"I have heard that a priest of pure life may gain power to see into the future for a hundred years; but truly this is the first time in my existence that I have had proof of such power... Still, there is another matter about which I am very anxious..."

"You mean," interrupted Ryoseki, "the stealing of the holy *mamori*, the *Kai-On-Nyorai*. But you must not give yourself any concern about that. The image has been buried in a field; and it will be found there and returned to me during the eighth month of the coming year. So please do not be anxious about it."

More and more amazed, the old *ninsomi* ventured to observe:

"I have studied the *In-Yo*,[17] and the science of divination; and I make my living by telling peoples' fortunes; but I cannot possibly understand how you know these things."

Ryoseki answered gravely:

"Never mind how I happen to know them.... I now want to speak to you about Hagiwara's funeral. The House of Hagiwara has its own family cemetery, of course; but to bury him there would not be proper. He must be buried beside O-Tsuyu, the Lady Iijima; for his karma relation to her was a very deep one. And it is but right that you should erect a tomb for him at your own cost, because you have been indebted to him for many favors."

Thus it came to pass that Shinzaburo was buried beside O-Tsuyu, in the cemetery of Shin-Banzui-In, in Yanaka-no-Sasaki.

Notes

1. The *hatamoto* were samurai forming the special military force of the Shogun. The name literally signifies "Banner Supporters." These were the highest class of samurai—not only as the immediate vassals of the Shogun, but as a military aristocracy.
2. Perhaps this conversation may seem strange to the Western reader; but it is true to life. The whole of the scene is characteristically Japanese.
3. The invocation *Namu Amida Butsu!* ("Hail to the Buddha Amitabha!"), repeated, as a prayer, for the sake of the dead.
4. *Komageta* in the original. The geta is a wooden sandal, or clog, of which there are many varieties, some decidedly elegant. The *komageta*, or "pony-geta" is so-called because of the sonorous hoof-like echo which it makes on hard ground.
5. The sort of lantern here referred to is no longer made. It was totally unlike the modern domestic band-lantern, painted with the owner's crest; but it was not altogether unlike some forms of lanterns still manufactured for the Festival of the Dead, and called *Bondoro*. The flowers ornamenting it were not painted: they were artificial flowers of crepe silk, and were attached to the top of the lantern.
6. "For the time of seven existences"—that is to say, for the time of seven successive lives. In Japanese drama and romance it is not uncommon to represent a father as disowning his child "for the time of seven lives." Such a disowning is called *shichi-sho made no mando*, a disinheritance for seven lives, signifying that in six future lives after the present the erring son or daughter will continue to feel the parental displeasure.
7. The profession is not yet extinct. The *ninsomi* uses a kind of magnifying glass (or magnifying mirror sometimes), called *tengankyo* or *ninsomegane*.
8. The color and form of the dress, and the style of wearing the hair, are by Japanese custom regulated according to the age of the woman.
9. The forms of speech used by the samurai, and other superior classes, differed considerably from those of the popular idiom; but these differences could not be effectively rendered into English.
10. The Japanese word *mamori* has significations at least as numerous as those attaching to our own term "amulet." It would be impossible, in a mere footnote, even to suggest the variety of Japanese religious objects to which the name is given. In this instance, the *mamori* is a very small image, probably enclosed in a miniature shrine of lacquerwork or metal, over which a silk cover is drawn. Such little images were often worn by samurai on the person. I was recently shown a miniature figure of Kwannon, in an iron case, which had been carried by an officer through the Satsuma war. He observed,

with good reason, that it had probably saved his life; for it had stopped a bullet of which the dent was plainly visible.

11. From *shiryo*, a ghost, and *yokeru*, to exclude. The Japanese have two kinds of ghosts proper in their folklore: the spirits of the dead, *shiryo*; and the spirits of the living, *ikiryo*. A house or a person may be haunted by an *ikiryo* as well as by a *shiryo*.

12. A special service—accompanying offerings of food, etc., to those dead having no living relatives or friends to care for them—is thus termed. In this case, however, the service would be of a particular and exceptional kind.

13. The name would be more correctly written *Ubo-Darani-Kyo*. It is the Japanese pronunciation of the title of a very short sutra translated out of Sanskrit into Chinese by the Indian priest Amoghavajra, probably during the eighth century. The Chinese text contains transliterations of some mysterious Sanskrit words—apparently talismanic words—like those to be seen in Kern's translation of the Saddharma-Pundarîka, ch. xxvi.

14. *O-fuda* is the general name given to religious texts used as charms or talismans. They are sometimes stamped or burned upon wood, but more commonly written or printed upon narrow strips of paper. *O-fuda* are pasted above house entrances, on the walls of rooms, upon tablets placed in household shrines, etc., etc. Some kinds are worn about the person; others are made into pellets, and swallowed as spiritual medicine. The text of the larger *o-fuda* is often accompanied by curious pictures or symbolic illustrations.

15. According to the old Japanese way of counting time, this *yatsudoki* or eighth hour was the same as our two o'clock in the morning. Each Japanese hour was equal to two European hours, so that there were only six hours instead of our twelve; and these six hours were counted backwards in the order—9, 8, 7, 6, 5, 4. Thus the ninth hour corresponded to our midday, or midnight; half-past nine to our one o'clock; eight to our two o'clock. Two o'clock in the morning, also called "the Hour of the Ox," was the Japanese hour of ghosts and goblins.

16. Ennetsu or Shonetsu (Sanskrit "Tapana") is the sixth of the Eight Hot Hells of Japanese Buddhism. One day of life in this hell is equal in duration to thousands (some say millions) of human years.

17. The Male and Female principles of the universe, the Active and Passive forces of Nature. Yusai refers here to the old Chinese nature philosophy, better known to Western readers by the name feng shui.

THE BAMBOO CUTTER AND THE MOON CHILD

Long, long ago, there lived an old bamboo woodcutter. He was very poor and sad also, for no child had Heaven sent to cheer his old age, and in his heart there was no hope of rest from work till he died and was laid in the quiet grave. Every morning he went forth into the woods and hills wherever the bamboo reared its lithe green plumes against the sky. When he had made his choice, he would cut down these feathers of the forest, and splitting them lengthwise, or cutting them into joints, would carry the bamboo wood home and make it into various articles for the household, and he and his old wife gained a small livelihood by selling them.

One morning as usual he had gone out to his work, and having found a nice clump of bamboo, had set to work to cut some of them down. Suddenly the green grove of bamboos was flooded with a bright soft light, as if the full moon had risen over the spot. Looking round in astonishment, he saw that the brilliance was streaming from one bamboo. The old man, full of wonder, dropped his ax and went towards the light. On nearer approach he saw that this soft splendor came from a hollow in the green bamboo stem, and still more wonderful to behold, in the midst of the brilliance stood a tiny human being, only three inches in height, and exquisitely beautiful in appearance.

"You must be sent to be my child, for I find you here among the bamboos where lies my daily work," said the old man, and taking the little creature in his hand he took it home to his wife to bring up. The tiny girl was so exceedingly beautiful and so small, that the old woman put her into a basket to safeguard her from the least possibility of being hurt in any way.

The old couple were now very happy, for it had been a lifelong regret that they had no children of their own, and with joy they now expended all the love of their old age on the little child who had come to them in so marvelous a manner.

From this time on, the old man often found gold in the notches of the bamboos when he hewed them down and cut them up; not only gold, but precious stones also, so that by degrees he became rich. He built himself a fine house, and was no longer known as the poor bamboo woodcutter, but as a wealthy man.

Three months passed quickly away, and in that time the bamboo child had, wonderful to say, become a full-grown girl, so her foster parents did up her hair and dressed her in beautiful kimonos. She was of such wondrous beauty that they placed her behind the screens like a princess, and allowed no one to see her, waiting upon her themselves. It seemed as if she were made of light, for the house was filled with a soft shining, so that even in the dark of night it was like daytime. Her presence seemed to have a benign influence on those there. Whenever the old man felt sad, he had only to look upon his foster daughter and his sorrow vanished, and he became as happy as when he was a youth.

At last the day came for the naming of their newfound child, so the old couple called in a celebrated name-giver, and he gave her the name of Princess Moonlight, because her body gave forth so much soft bright light that she might have been a daughter of the Moon God.

For three days the festival was kept up with song and dance and music. All the friends and relations of the old couple were present, and great was their enjoyment of the festivities held to celebrate the naming of Princess Moonlight. Everyone who saw her declared that there never had been seen any one so lovely; all the beauties throughout the length and breadth of the land would grow pale beside her, so they said. The fame of the Princess's loveliness spread far and wide, and many were the suitors who desired to win her hand, or even so much as to see her.

Suitors from far and near posted themselves outside the house, and made little holes in the fence, in the hope of catching a glimpse of the Princess as she went from one room to the other along the veranda. They stayed there day and night, sacrificing even their sleep for a chance of seeing her, but all in vain. Then they approached the house, and tried to speak to the old man and his wife or some of the servants, but not even this was granted them.

Still, in spite of all this disappointment they stayed on day after day, and night after night, and counted it as nothing, so great was their desire to see the Princess.

At last, however, most of the men, seeing how hopeless their quest was, lost heart and hope both, and returned to their homes. All except five Knights, whose ardor and determination, instead of waning, seemed to wax greater with obstacles. These five men even went without their meals, and took snatches of whatever they could get brought to them, so that they might always stand outside the dwelling. They stood there in all weathers, in sunshine and in rain.

Sometimes they wrote letters to the Princess, but no answer was vouchsafed to them. Then when letters failed to draw any reply, they wrote poems to her telling her of the hopeless love which kept them from sleep, from food, from rest, and even from their homes. Still Princess Moonlight gave no sign of having received their verses.

In this hopeless state the winter passed. The snow and frost and the cold winds gradually gave place to the gentle warmth of spring. Then the summer came, and the sun burned white and scorching in the heavens above and on the earth beneath, and still these faithful Knights kept watch and waited. At the end of these long months they called out to the old bamboo cutter and entreated him to have some mercy upon them and to show them the Princess, but he answered only that as he was not her real father he could not insist on her obeying him against her wishes.

The five Knights on receiving this stern answer returned to their several homes, and pondered over the best means of touching the proud Princess's heart, even so much as to grant them a hearing. They took their rosaries in hand and knelt before their household shrines, and burned precious incense, praying to Buddha to give them their heart's desire. Thus several days passed, but even so they could not rest in their homes.

So again they set out for the bamboo cutter's house. This time the old man came out to see them, and they asked him to let them know if it was the Princess's resolution never to see any man whatsoever, and they implored him to speak for them and to tell her the greatness of their love, and how long they had waited through the cold of winter and the heat of summer, sleepless and roofless through all weathers, without food and without rest, in the ardent hope of winning her, and they were willing to consider this long vigil as pleasure if she would but give them one chance of pleading their cause with her.

The old man lent a willing ear to their tale of love, for in his innermost heart he felt sorry for these faithful suitors and would have liked to see his lovely foster daughter married to one of them. So he went in to Princess Moonlight and said reverently:

"Although you have always seemed to me to be a heavenly being, yet I have had the trouble of bringing you up as my own child and you have been glad of the protection of my roof. Will you refuse to do as I wish?"

Then Princess Moonlight replied that there was nothing she would not do for him, that she honored and loved him as her own father, and that as for herself she could not remember the time before she came to earth.

The old man listened with great joy as she spoke these dutiful words. Then he told her how anxious he was to see her safely and happily married before he died.

"I am an old man, over seventy years of age, and my end may come any time now. It is necessary and right that you should see these five suitors and choose one of them."

"Oh, why," said the Princess in distress, "must I do this? I have no wish to marry now."

"I found you," answered the old man, "many years ago, when you were a little creature three inches high, in the midst of a great white light. The light streamed from the bamboo in which you were hid and led me to you. So I have always thought that you were more than mortal woman. While I am alive it is right for you to remain as you are if you wish to do so, but some day I shall cease to be and who will take care of you then? Therefore I pray you to meet these five brave men one at a time and make up your mind to marry one of them!"

Then the Princess answered that she felt sure that she was not as beautiful as perhaps report made her out to be, and that even if she consented to marry any one of them, not really knowing her before, his heart might change afterwards. So as she did not feel sure of them, even though her father told her they were worthy Knights, she did not feel it wise to see them.

"All you say is very reasonable," said the old man, "but what kind of men will you consent to see? I do not call these five men who have waited on you for months lighthearted. They have stood outside this house through the winter and the summer, often denying themselves food and sleep so that they may win you. What more can you demand?"

Then Princess Moonlight said she must make further trial of their love before she would grant their request to interview her. The five warriors were to prove their love by each bringing her from distant countries something that she desired to possess.

That same evening the suitors arrived and began to play their flutes in turn, and to sing their self-composed songs telling of their great and tireless love. The bamboo cutter went out to them and offered them his sympathy for all they had endured and all the patience they had shown in their desire to win his foster daughter. Then he gave them her message, that she would consent to marry whosoever was successful in bringing her what she wanted. This was to test them.

The five all accepted the trial, and thought it an excellent plan, for it would prevent jealousy between them.

Princess Moonlight then sent word to the First Knight that she requested him to bring her the stone bowl which had belonged to Buddha in India.

The Second Knight was asked to go to the Mountain of Horai, said to be situated in the Eastern Sea, and to bring her a branch of the wonderful tree that grew on its summit. The roots of this tree were of silver, the trunk of gold, and the branches bore as fruit white jewels.

The Third Knight was told to go to China and search for the fire-rat and to bring her its skin.

The Fourth Knight was told to search for the dragon that carried on its head the stone radiating five colors and to bring the stone to her.

The Fifth Knight was to find the swallow which carried a shell in its stomach and to bring the shell to her.

The old man thought these very hard tasks and hesitated to carry the messages, but the Princess would make no other conditions. So her commands were issued word for word to the five men who, when they heard what was required of them, were all disheartened and disgusted at what seemed to them the impossibility of the tasks given them and returned to their own homes in despair.

But after a time, when they thought of the Princess, the love in their hearts revived for her, and they resolved to make an attempt to get what she desired of them.

The First Knight sent word to the Princess that he was starting out that day on the quest of Buddha's bowl, and he hoped soon to bring it to her. But he had not the courage to go all the way to India, for in those days traveling was very difficult and full of danger, so he went to one of the temples in Kyoto and took a stone bowl from the altar there, paying the priest a large sum of money for it. He then wrapped it in a cloth of gold and, waiting quietly for three years, returned and carried it to the old man.

Princess Moonlight wondered that the Knight should have returned so soon. She took the bowl from its gold wrapping, expecting it to make the room full of light, but it did not shine at all, so she knew that it was a sham thing and not the true bowl of Buddha. She returned it at once and refused to see him. The Knight threw the bowl away and returned to his home in despair. He gave up now all hopes of ever winning the Princess.

The Second Knight told his parents that he needed change of air for his health, for he was ashamed to tell them that love for the Princess Moonlight was the real cause of his leaving them. He then left his home, at the same time sending word to the Princess that he was setting out for Mount Horai in the hope of getting her a branch of the gold and silver tree which she so much wished to have. He only allowed his servants to accompany him halfway, and then sent them back. He reached the seashore and embarked on a small ship, and after sailing away for three days he landed and employed several carpenters to build him a house contrived in such a way that no one could get access to it. He then shut himself up with six skilled jewelers, and endeavored to make such a gold and silver branch as he thought would satisfy the Princess as having come from the wonderful tree growing on Mount Horai. Every one whom he had asked declared that Mount Horai belonged to the land of fable and not to fact.

When the branch was finished, he took his journey home and tried to make himself look as if he were wearied and worn out with travel. He put the jeweled branch into a lacquer box and carried it to the bamboo cutter, begging him to present it to the Princess.

The old man was quite deceived by the travel-stained appearance of the Knight, and thought that he had only just returned from his long journey with the branch. So he tried to persuade the Princess to consent to see the man. But she remained silent and looked very sad. The old man began to take out the branch and praised it as a wonderful treasure to be found nowhere in the whole land. Then he spoke of the Knight, how handsome and how brave he was to have undertaken a journey to so remote a place as the Mount of Horai.

Princess Moonlight took the branch in her hand and looked at it carefully. She then told her foster parent that she knew it was impossible for the man to have obtained a branch from the gold and silver tree growing on Mount Horai so quickly or so easily, and she was sorry to say she believed it artificial.

The old man then went out to the expectant Knight, who had now approached the house, and asked where he had found the branch. Then the man did not scruple to make up a long story.

"Two years ago I took a ship and started in search of Mount Horai. After going before the wind for some time I reached the far Eastern Sea. Then a great storm arose and I was tossed about for many days, losing all count of the points of the compass, and finally we were blown ashore on an unknown island. Here I found the place inhabited by demons who at one time threatened to kill and eat me. However, I managed to make friends with these horrible creatures, and they helped me and my sailors to repair the boat, and I set sail again. Our food gave out, and we suffered much from sickness on board. At last, on the five-hundredth day from the day of starting, I saw far off on the horizon what looked like the peak of a mountain. On nearer approach, this proved to be an island, in the center of which rose a high mountain. I landed, and after wandering about for two or three days, I saw a shining being coming towards me on the beach, holding in his hands a golden bowl. I went up to him and asked him if I had, by good chance, found the island of Mount Horai, and he answered:

"'Yes, this is Mount Horai!'"

"With much difficulty I climbed to the summit, here stood the golden tree growing with silver roots in the ground. The wonders of that strange land are many, and if I began to tell you about them I could never stop. In spite of my wish to stay there long, on breaking off the branch I hurried back. With utmost speed it has taken me four hundred days to get back, and, as you see, my clothes are still damp from exposure on the long sea voyage. I have not even waited to change my raiment, so anxious was I to bring the branch to the Princess quickly."

Just at this moment the six jewelers, who had been employed on the making of the branch, but not yet paid by the Knight, arrived at the house and sent in a petition to the Princess to be paid for their labor. They said that they had worked for over a thousand days making the branch of gold, with its silver twigs and its jeweled fruit, that was now presented to her by the Knight, but as yet they had received nothing in payment. So this Knight's deception was thus found out, and the Princess, glad of an escape from one more importunate suitor, was only too pleased to send back the branch. She called in the work-men and had them paid liberally, and they went away happy. But on the way home they were overtaken by the disappointed man, who beat them till they were nearly dead, for letting out the secret, and they barely escaped with their lives. The Knight then returned home, raging in his heart; and in despair of ever winning the Princess gave up society and retired to a solitary life among the mountains.

Now the Third Knight had a friend in China, so he wrote to him to get the skin of the fire-rat. The virtue of any part of this animal was that no fire could harm it. He promised his friend any amount of money he liked to ask if only he could get him the desired article. As soon as the news came that the ship on which his friend had sailed home had come into port, he rode seven days on horseback to meet him. He handed his friend a large sum of money, and received the fire-rat's skin. When he reached home he put it carefully in a box and sent it in to the Princess while he waited outside for her answer.

The bamboo cutter took the box from the Knight and, as usual, carried it in to her and tried to coax her to see the Knight at once, but Princess Moon-light refused, saying that she must first put the skin to test by putting it into the fire. If it were the real thing it would not burn. So she took off the crape wrapper and opened the box, and then threw the skin into the fire. The skin crackled and burnt up at once, and the Princess knew that this man also had not fulfilled his word. So the Third Knight failed also.

Now the Fourth Knight was no more enterprising than the rest. Instead of starting out on the quest of the dragon bearing on its head the five-color radiating jewel, he called all his servants together and gave them the order to seek for it far and wide in Japan and in China, and he strictly forbade any of them to return till they had found it.

His numerous retainers and servants started out in different directions, with no intention, however, of obeying what they considered an impossible order. They simply took a holiday, went to pleasant country places together, and grumbled at their master's unreasonableness.

The Knight meanwhile, thinking that his retainers could not fail to find the jewel, repaired to his house, and fitted it up beautifully for the reception of the Princess, he felt so sure of winning her.

One year passed away in weary waiting, and still his men did not return with the dragon-jewel. The Knight became desperate. He could wait no longer, so taking with him only two men he hired a ship and commanded the captain to go in search of the dragon; the captain and the sailors refused to undertake what they said was an absurd search, but the Knight compelled them at last to put out to sea.

When they had been but a few days out they encountered a great storm which lasted so long that, by the time its fury abated, the Knight had determined to give up the hunt of the dragon. They were at last blown on shore, for navigation was primitive in those days. Worn out with his travels and anxiety, the fourth suitor gave himself up to rest. He had caught a very heavy cold, and had to go to bed with a swollen face.

The governor of the place, hearing of his plight, sent messengers with a letter inviting him to his house. While he was there thinking over all his troubles, his love for the Princess turned to anger, and he blamed her for all the hardships he had undergone. He thought that it was quite probable she had wished to kill him so that she might be rid of him, and in order to carry out her wish had sent him upon his impossible quest.

At this point all the servants he had sent out to find the jewel came to see him, and were surprised to find praise instead of displeasure awaiting them. Their master told them that he was heartily sick of adventure, and said that he never intended to go near the Princess's house again in the future.

Like all the rest, the Fifth Knight failed in his quest—he could not find the swallow's shell.

By this time the fame of Princess Moonlight's beauty had reached the ears of the Emperor, and he sent one of the Court ladies to see if she were really as lovely as report said; if so he would summon her to the Palace and make her one of the ladies-in-waiting.

When the Court lady arrived, in spite of her father's entreaties, Princess Moonlight refused to see her. The Imperial messenger insisted, saying it was the Emperor's order. Then Princess Moonlight told the old man that if she was forced to go to the Palace in obedience to the Emperor's order, she would vanish from the earth.

When the Emperor was told of her persistence in refusing to obey his summons, and that if pressed to obey she would disappear altogether from sight, he determined to go and see her. So he planned to go on a hunting excursion in the neighborhood of the bamboo cutter's house, and see the Princess himself. He sent word to the old man of his intention, and he received consent to the scheme. The next day the Emperor set out with his retinue, which he soon managed to outride. He found the bamboo cutter's house and dismounted. He then entered the house and went straight to where the Princess was sitting with her attendant maidens.

Never had he seen any one so wonderfully beautiful, and he could not but look at her, for she was more lovely than any human being as she shone in her own soft radiance. When Princess Moonlight became aware that a stranger was looking at her she tried to escape from the room, but the Emperor caught her and begged her to listen to what he had to say. Her only answer was to hide her face in her sleeves.

The Emperor fell deeply in love with her, and begged her to come to the Court, where he would give her a position of honor and everything she could wish for. He was about to send for one of the Imperial palanquins to take her back with him at once, saying that her grace and beauty should adorn a Court, and not be hidden in a bamboo cutter's cottage.

But the Princess stopped him. She said that if she were forced to go to the Palace she would turn at once into a shadow, and even as she spoke she began to lose her form. Her figure faded from his sight while he looked.

The Emperor then promised to leave her free if only she would resume her former shape, which she did.

It was now time for him to return, for his retinue would be wondering what had happened to their Royal master when they missed him for so long. So he bade her goodbye, and left the house with a sad heart. Princess Moonlight was for him the most beautiful woman in the world; all others were dark beside her, and he thought of her night and day. His Majesty now spent much of his time in writing poems, telling her of his love and devotion, and sent them to her, and though she refused to see him again she answered with many verses of her own composing, which told him gently and kindly that she could never marry any one on this earth. These little songs always gave him pleasure.

At this time her foster parents noticed that night after night the Princess would sit on her balcony and gaze for hours at the moon, in a spirit of the deepest dejection, ending always in a burst of tears. One night the old man found her thus weeping as if her heart were broken, and he besought her to tell him the reason of her sorrow.

With many tears she told him that he had guessed rightly when he supposed her not to belong to this world—that she had in truth come from the moon, and that her time on earth would soon be over. On the fifteenth day of that very month of August her friends from the moon would come to fetch her, and she would have to return. Her parents were both there, but having spent a lifetime on the earth she had forgotten them, and also the moon-world to which she belonged. It made her weep, she said, to think of leaving her kind foster parents, and the home where she had been happy for so long.

When her attendants heard this they were very sad, and could not eat or drink for sadness at the thought that the Princess was so soon to leave them.

The Emperor, as soon as the news was carried to him, sent messengers to the house to find out if the report were true or not.

The old bamboo cutter went out to meet the Imperial messengers. The last few days of sorrow had told upon the old man; he had aged greatly, and looked much more than his seventy years. Weeping bitterly, he told them that the report was only too true, but he intended, however, to make prisoners of the envoys from the moon, and to do all he could to prevent the Princess from being carried back.

The men returned and told His Majesty all that had passed. On the fifteenth day of that month the Emperor sent a guard of two thousand warriors to watch the house. One thousand stationed themselves on the roof, another thousand kept watch round all the entrances of the house. All were well trained archers, with bows and arrows. The bamboo cutter and his wife hid Princess Moonlight in an inner room.

The old man gave orders that no one was to sleep that night, all in the house were to keep a strict watch, and be ready to protect the Princess. With these precautions, and the help of the Emperor's men-at-arms, he hoped to withstand the moon-messengers, but the Princess told him that all these measures to keep her would be useless, and that when her people came for her nothing whatever could prevent them from carrying out their purpose. Even the Emperor's men would be powerless. Then she added with tears that she was very, very sorry to leave him and his wife, whom she had learned to love as her parents, that if she could do as she liked she would stay with them in their old age, and try to make some return for all the love and kindness they had showered upon her during all her earthly life.

The night wore on! The yellow harvest moon rose high in the heavens, flooding the world asleep with her golden light. Silence reigned over the pine and the bamboo forests, and on the roof where the thousand men-at-arms waited.

Then the night grew gray towards the dawn and all hoped that the danger was over—that Princess Moonlight would not have to leave them after all. Then suddenly the watchers saw a cloud form round the moon—and while they looked this cloud began to roll earthwards. Nearer and nearer it came, and every one saw with dismay that its course lay towards the house.

In a short time the sky was entirely obscured, till at last the cloud lay over the dwelling only ten feet off the ground. In the midst of the cloud there stood a flying chariot, and in the chariot a band of luminous beings. One amongst them who looked like a king and appeared to be the chief stepped out of the chariot, and, poised in air, called to the old man to come out.

"The time has come," he said, "for Princess Moonlight to return to the moon from whence she came. She committed a grave fault, and as a punishment was sent to live down here for a time. We know what good care you have taken of the Princess, and we have rewarded you for this and have sent you wealth and prosperity. We put the gold in the bamboo for you to find."

"I have brought up this Princess for twenty years and never once has she done a wrong thing, therefore the lady you are seeking cannot be this one," said the old man. "I pray you to look elsewhere."

Then the messenger called aloud, saying:

"Princess Moonlight, come out from this lowly dwelling. Rest not here another moment."

At these words the screens of the Princess's room slid open of their own accord, revealing the Princess shining in her own radiance, bright and wonderful and full of beauty.

The messenger led her forth and placed her in the chariot. She looked back, and saw with pity the deep sorrow of the old man. She spoke to him many comforting words, and told him that it was not her will to leave him and that he must always think of her when looking at the moon.

The bamboo cutter implored to be allowed to accompany her, but this was not allowed. The Princess took off her embroidered outer garment and gave it to him as a keepsake.

One of the moon beings in the chariot held a wonderful coat of wings, another had a phial full of the Elixir of Life which was given the Princess to drink. She swallowed a little and was about to give the rest to the old man, but she was prevented from doing so.

The robe of wings was about to be put upon her shoulders, but she said:

"Wait a little. I must not forget my good friend the Emperor. I must write him once more to say goodbye while still in this human form."

In spite of the impatience of the messengers and charioteers she kept them waiting while she wrote. She placed the phial of the Elixir of Life with the letter, and, giving them to the old man, she asked him to deliver them to the Emperor.

Then the chariot began to roll heavenwards towards the moon, and as they all gazed with tearful eyes at the receding Princess, the dawn broke, and in the rosy light of day the moon-chariot and all in it were lost amongst the fleecy clouds that were now wafted across the sky on the wings of the morning wind.

Princess Moonlight's letter was carried to the Palace. His Majesty was afraid to touch the Elixir of Life, so he sent it with the letter to the top of the most sacred mountain in the land, Mount Fuji, and there the Royal emissaries burnt it on the summit at sunrise. So to this day people say there is smoke to be seen rising from the top of Mount Fuji to the clouds.

THE GOBLIN
OF OEYAMA

Long, long ago in Old Japan, in the reign of the Emperor Ichijo, the
sixty-sixth Emperor, there lived a very brave general called Minamoto-no-Raiko. Minamoto was the name of the powerful clan to which
he belonged, and in England it would be called his surname, and Raiko, or
Yorimitsu,[1] was his own name.

In those times it was the custom for generals to keep as a bodyguard four
picked knights renowned for their daring spirit, their great strength, and their
skill in wielding the sword. These four braves were called Shitenno, or Four
Kings of Heaven, and they participated in all the exploits and martial expeditions
of their chief, and vied with one another in excelling in bravery and dexterity.

Minamoto-no-Raiko was no exception to the general rule of those ancient
leaders of Japan, and he had under him Usui-Sadamitsu, Sakata Kintoki, Urabe
Suetake, and Watanabe Tsuna (the clan or surname comes first in Japan).
Search the wide world from north to south and from east to west, and no
braver warriors than the Shitenno of Minamoto-no-Raiko could you find. Each

one of the four was said to be a match single-handed for a thousand men. They lived for adventure, and their delight was in war.

Now it happened about this time that Kyoto, the capital, was ringing with the stories of the doings of a frightful demon that lived in the fastnesses of a high mountain called Mount Oe, in the province of Tamba. This goblin or demon's name was Shutendoji. To look upon the creature was a horrible thing, and those who once caught sight of him never forgot the sight to their dying day. He sometimes took upon him the form of a human being, and leaving his den would steal into the capital and haunt the streets and carry off precious sons and beloved daughters of the Kyoto homes. Having seized these treasures and flowers of the people, he would drag them to his castle in the wilds of Mount Oe, and there he would make them work and wait upon him till he was ready to devour them, then he would tear them limb from limb.

For a long time the flower of the youth of the capital had been kidnapped in this way; many homes had been made desolate. For a long, long time no one had the least idea of what happened to the sons and daughters thus stolen, but at the period when this story begins, the dread news of the cannibal Shutendoji and his mountain den began to be noised abroad.

Now at the Court there was an official, Knight Kimitaka by name, who was thrice happy in the possession of a beautiful daughter. She was his only child, and upon her he and his wife doted. One day the darling of the family disappeared, and no trace whatsoever of the beautiful girl could be found. The household was plunged into the deepest grief and misery. The mother at last determined to consult a soothsayer, and, bidding an attendant follow her, she repaired to the house of a famous fortune teller and diviner, who revealed to her that her daughter had been stolen away by the goblin of Mount Oe. The mother hastened home terror-stricken, and the father, when he was told the dire news, was dumb with grief. He gave up going on duty at the Palace, for he was so broken-hearted that he could do nothing but weep night and day over the loss of his only daughter. To lose her was bad enough, but the thought of the horrible hands into which she had fallen was unendurable, and all who loved the poor child, even her own father, were powerless to save her. Oh! the bitter, bitter grief!

At last the Emperor heard of the sorrow that had overtaken Kimitaka, and his wrath was great to think that the hateful goblin had dared to enter the precincts of the sacred capital without permission, and had dared to steal away his subjects in this manner. And in his royal indignation he sprang to his feet and threw down his tasseled fan and cried aloud: "Is there no one in my domains who will punish this goblin and destroy him utterly, and avenge the wrongs he has done my people and this city, and so set my heart at ease?"

Then the Emperor called his Council together, and put the matter before them and asked them what it were best to do, for the city must at all costs be rid of this terrible scourge.

"How dare he haunt my dominions and lay hands on my people in the very precincts of my Palace?" cried the distressed Emperor.

Then the Ministers respectfully answered the Emperor and said: "There are numbers of brave warriors in Your Majesty's realm, but there are none so able to do your bidding as Minamoto-no-Raiko. We would humbly advise our August Emperor, the Son of Heaven, to send for the knight and command him to slay the demon. Our poor counsel may not find favor in the Son of Heaven's sight, but at the present moment we can think of nothing else to suggest!"

This advice pleased the Emperor Ichijo, and he answered that he had often heard of Raiko as a valiant knight and true, who knew not what fear was, and he had no doubt that, as his Ministers said, he was just the man for the adventure. And so the Emperor summoned Raiko to the Palace at once.

The warrior, on receiving the royal and unexpected summons, hastened to the Palace, wondering what it could mean. When he was told what was wanted of him, he prostrated himself before the throne in humble acquiescence to the royal command. Indeed Raiko was right glad at the thought of the adventure in store for him, for it had been quiet for some time in Kyoto, and he and his braves had chafed at the enforced idleness.

The more he realized the awful difficulty of his task, the higher his courage and his spirits rose to face it and the more he determined to do it or die in the attempt.

He went home and thought out a plan of action.

As the enemy was no human being, but a formidable goblin, he thought that the wisest course would be to resort to stratagem instead of an open encounter, so he decided to take with him a few of his most trusted men rather than a great number of soldiers. He then called together his four braves, Kintoki, Sadamitsu, Suetake, and Tsuna, and besides these another knight, by name Hirai Yasumasa, nicknamed Hitori, which meant, as applied to him, "the only warrior."

Raiko told them of the expedition, and explained that, as the demon was no common foe, he thought it wise that they should go to his mountain in disguise; in this way they would the more likely and the more easily overcome the goblin. They all agreed to what their chief said and set about making their preparations with great joy. They polished up their armor and sharpened their long swords and tried on their helmets, rejoicing in the prospect of the action confronting them. Before starting on this dangerous enterprise, they thought it wise to seek the protection and blessing of the gods, so Raiko and Yasumasa went to pray for help at the Temple of Hachiman, the God of War, at Mount Otoko, while Tsuna and Kintoki went to the Sumiyoshi Shrine of the Goddess of Mercy, and Sadamitsu and Suetake to the Temple of Gongen at Kumano. At each shrine the six knights offered up the same prayer for divine help and strength, and on bended knees and with hands laid palm to palm they besought the gods to grant them success in their expedition and a safe return to the capital.

Then the brave band disguised themselves as mountain priests. They wore priests' caps and sacerdotal garments and stoles; they hid their armor and their helmets and their weapons in the knapsacks they carried on their backs; in their right hands they carried a pilgrim's staff, and in their left a rosary, and they wore rough straw sandals on their feet. No one meeting these dignified, solemn-looking priests would have thought that they were on the way to attack the goblin of Mount Oe, and no one would have dreamt that the leader of the band was the warrior Raiko, who for courage and strength had not his peer in the whole of the Island Empire.

In this way Raiko and his men travelled across the country till at last they reached the province of Tamba and came to the foot of the mountain of Oe. Now as the goblin had chosen Mount Oe as his place of abode, you can imagine how difficult of access it was! Raiko and his men had often traveled in mountainous districts, but they had never experienced anything like the steepness of Mount Oe. It was indescribable. Great rocks obstructed the way, and the branches of the trees were so thickly interlaced overhead that the light of day could not penetrate through the foliage even at midday, and the shadows were so black that the warriors would have been glad of lanterns. Sometimes the path led them over precipices where they could hear the water rushing along the deep ravines beneath. So deep were these chasms that as Raiko and his men passed them they were overcome with giddiness. For the first time they realized now the dangers and difficulties of the task they had undertaken, and they were somewhat disheartened. At times they rested themselves on the roots of trees to gain breath, sometimes they stopped to quench their thirst at some trickling spring, catching the water up in their hands. They did not, however, allow themselves to be discouraged long, but pushed their way deeper and deeper into the mountain, encouraging each other with brave words of cheer when they felt their spirits flagging. But the thought sometimes crossed their minds, though they one and all kept it to themselves, "What if Shutendoji, or some of his demons, should be lurking behind any of the rocks or cliffs?"

Suddenly from behind a rock three old men appeared. Now Raiko, who was as wise as he was brave, and who at that very moment had been think-ing of what he should do were they to encounter the goblin unexpectedly, thought that sure enough here were some of the goblins, who had heard of his approach. They had simply disguised themselves as these venerable old men so as to deceive him and his men! But he was not to be outwitted by any such prank. He made signs with his eyes to the men behind him to be on their guard, and they in obedience to his gesture put themselves in attitudes of defense.

The three old men saw at once the mistake Raiko had made, for they smiled at him and then drawing nearer, they bowed before him, and the foremost one said: "Do not be afraid of us; we are not the goblins of this mountain. I am from the province of Settsu. My friend is from Kii, and the third lives near the capital. We have all been bereft of our beloved wives and daughters by Shutendoji the goblin. Because of our great age we can do nothing to help them, though our sorrow for their loss, instead of growing less, grows greater day by day. We have heard of your coming, and we have awaited you here, so that we might ask you to help us in our distress. It is a great favor we ask, but we entreat you if you encounter Shutendoji to show him no mercy, but to slay him and so avenge the wrongs of our wives and children and many others who have been torn away from their homes in the Flower Capital."

Raiko listened attentively to all the old man said, and then answered: "Now that you have told me so much, I need not reserve the truth from you"; and he went on to tell them of the order he had received from the Emperor to destroy Shutendoji and his den, and the warrior did his best to comfort the old men and to assure them that he would do all in his power to restore their kidnapped wives and daughters.

Then the old men expressed great joy; their faces beamed like the sun as they thanked Raiko warmly for his kind sympathy, and they presented him with a jar of sake, saying as they bowed low: "As a token of our gratitude we wish to present you with this magic wine. It is called Shimben-Kidoku-Shu. The name means, 'a cordial for men but a poison to goblins.' Therefore if a demon drinks of this wine, all his strength will go from him, and he will be as one paralyzed. Before you attack Shutendoji, give him to drink of this wine, and for the rest you will find no difficulty."

And with these words the venerable spokesman handed the warrior a small white stone jar containing the wine. As soon as Raiko had taken the jar into his hands, a radiance like that of sunlight suddenly shone round the old men, and they vanished upwards from sight till their shining figures were lost in the clouds.

The warriors were struck with astonishment. They gazed upwards as if stupefied. But Raiko was the first to recover from his surprise. He clapped his hands and laughed as he said: "Be not afraid at what you have seen! Be sure that the three who thus appeared to us are none other than the gods of the shrines we visited before starting on this perilous enterprise. The old man who said he was from Settsu must have been the deity of Sumiyoshi, the one from the province of Kii was the divinity of Kumano, and the one from the capital the god Hachiman of Mount Otoko. This is a most propitious sign. The three deities have taken us under their special protection. This sake is their gift, and it will surely be of magic power in helping us to overcome the demons. We must, therefore, render thanks to Heaven for the protection vouchsafed to us."

Then Raiko and his five knights knelt down on the mountain pass and bowed themselves to the ground and prayed for some minutes in silence, overcome with awe at the thought that the three gods whose aid they had invoked had visited them. Raiko sprang to his feet and lifted the jar of sake reverently above his head, then he placed it with his armor and weapons in the box he carried on his back. Having done this, they all proceeded on their way, but oh! how safe and confident they now felt. Raiko with his magic wine felt more than a match for any demon now. There is a proverb which says, "A giant with an iron rod," which means strength added to strength, and this was fully illustrated in the case of Raiko. The goblin Shutendoji was now to be pitied; it would surely go hard with him!

As they sped on their way they came to a mountain stream, and here they found a damsel washing a blood-stained garment, and as she washed and beat the garment against the current, they saw that she often had to stop and wipe the tears away with her sleeve, for she was weeping bitterly. Raiko's heart was stirred with pity at her distress, and he went up to her and said: "This is a goblin-haunted mountain; how is it that I find a damsel such as you here?"

The Princess (for such she was) looked up in his face wonderingly and said: "It is indeed true that this is a goblin-haunted mountain, and hitherto inaccessible to mortals. How is it that you have managed to get here?" and she looked from Raiko to his men.

Then Raiko said: "I will tell you the truth quite frankly. The Emperor has commanded us to slay the demon; that is why we are here!"

Without waiting to hear any more, the Princess ran up to Raiko in her joy and clung to him, crying out in broken sentences: "Are you indeed the great Raiko of whom I have so often heard? How thankful I am that you have come. I will be your guide to the goblin's den. Hasten, Knight Raiko, and kill the demons! I already feel that I am saved!"

When they heard these words the warriors knew that she was one of the goblin's victims. The Princess turned and led the way up the hill. Presently they saw a large iron gate guarded by two demons. The demon on the right was red and the demon on the left was black, and each was armed with a great iron stick or club. The Princess whispered to Raiko: "Behold the home of the demon. Enter the gates, and you will find a beautiful palace, built of black iron from the foundations to the roof. It is therefore called the Palace of Black Iron or Kurogane. It is large, and the inside is as beautiful as a great daimyo's palace. Within the walls of the Palace of Black Iron, Shutendoji holds a feast night and day. He is waited upon by maidens such as I, whom he has carried off from the capital and from the provinces to be his slaves. The wine he drinks, poured out in crimson lacquer cups, is the blood of human beings, and the food of those feasts is the flesh of his victims who are slain in turn. What numbers have I seen disappear, alas! All murdered to supply the awful food and wine of those cannibal feasts. How I have prayed to Heaven to punish this monster! But when I saw the fate of my friends, how could I hope to live? I knew not when my turn would come. But since I have met you I feel that we shall all be saved and great is my joy and gratitude!"

By this time they had reached the gate, and the Princess went forward and said to the red and black demon sentinels: "These poor travelers have lost their way on this mountain. I took compassion on them and brought them here, so that they may rest for a while before going on their journey. I hope you will be kind to them."

When the Princess first began to speak the demons looked and saw Raiko and his fellow priests. Little dreaming who these men were, and that in admitting them they were letting in the bravest knights in the whole of Japan, and still less suspecting their purpose, the demons laughed in their hearts. Good prey had indeed fallen into their hands; they would surely be allowed a share in the feast that these fresh victims would furnish.

They grinned from ear to ear at the Princess and told her that she had done well, and bade her take the six travelers into the Palace and inform Shuten-doji of their arrival. Thus the six warriors entered into the very stronghold of the demons as if they were invited guests. Triumphant glee at the success of their plan made them exchange lightning glances with each other. They passed through the great iron gate, up to the porch, and then the Princess led them through large spacious rooms and along great corridors till at last they reached the inner part of the Palace. Here they were shown into a large hall. At the upper end in the seat of honor sat the demon king Shutendoji. Never had the knights in their wildest dreams dreamt of such a hideous monster. He was ten feet in height, his skin was bright red and his wild shock of hair was like a broom. He wore a crimson hakama,[2] and he rested his huge arms on a stand. As the knights entered, he glared at them fiercely with eyes as big as a dish. The sight of this dread monster was enough to make any one tremble with fear, and had Raiko and his knights been weak they must have fainted away with horror.

Raiko could hardly restrain himself from flying at the monster then and there, but he controlled himself and bowed humbly so as not to awaken the enemy's suspicion in any way.

Shutendoji, glaring at him, said haughtily: "I do not know who you are in the least, or how you have found your way into this mountain, but make yourself at home!"

Then Raiko answered meekly: "We are only humble mountain priests from Mount Haguro of Dewa. We were on our way to the capital, having been on a pilgrimage to the shrine of Omine. In traveling across these mountains we have lost our way. While wandering about and wondering which was the right path to take, we were met by one of the inmates of your palace and kindly brought here. Please pardon us for trespassing on your domains and for all the trouble we are giving you!"

"Don't mention it," said Shutendoji; "I am sorry to hear of your plight. Do not stand on ceremony while you are here, and let us feast together." Then turning to the attendant demons he shouted orders for the dinner to be served, and clapped his red hands together.

At this the partitions between the rooms slid apart and beautiful damsels magnificently robed came gliding in, bearing aloft in their hands large wine cups, jars of sake and dishes of fish of all kinds, which they placed before the ugly goblin and the guests. Raiko knew that all these lovely princesses had been snatched from the Flower Capital by Shutendoji, who, heedless of their tears and misery, kept them here to be his handmaidens. He said to himself fiercely that they should soon be free.

Now that the wine cups were brought in, the warrior seized his opportunity. From his satchel he took out the jar containing the enchanted wine, Shim-ben-Kidoku-Shu, which he had received from the gods of the three shrines, and said to Shutendoji: "Here is some wine which we have brought from Mount Haguro. It is a poor wine and unworthy of your acceptance, but we have always found it of great benefit in refreshing us when we were weary from fatigue and in cheering our drooping spirits. It will give us much pleasure if you will try a little of our humble wine, though it may not please your taste!"

Shutendoji seemed pleased at this courtesy. He handed out a huge cup to be filled, saying: "Give me some of your wine. I should like to try it." The goblin drained it at one swallow and smacked his lips over it.

"I have never tasted such excellent wine," he said and held out his cup to be filled again.

You can imagine how delighted Raiko was, for he knew full well that the demon was given into his hand. But he dissembled cleverly and said as he filled the goblin's wine cup: "I am delighted that the Honorable Host should deign to like our poor country wine. While you drink, I and my companions will venture to amuse you by our dancing."

Then Raiko made a sign to his men and they began to chant an accompaniment, while he himself danced.

Shutendoji was highly amused as well as his attendants. They had never seen men dance before, and they thought that the strangers were very entertaining.

The goblins now began to pass the magic wine round and to grow merry. Others meanwhile whispered among themselves, pitying the six travelers who, all unconscious of the horrible fate which was about to overtake them, were spending their last hours of liberty and probably of life in giving wine to their slayers and in dancing and singing for their amusement!

Already, however, the power of the enchanted wine had begun to work and Shutendoji grew drowsy. The wine in the jar never seemed to grow less, however much was taken from it, and by this time all the demons had helped themselves liberally. At last they all fell into a deep sleep, and stretching themselves out on the floor and on one another, some in one corner and some in another, they were soon snoring so loudly that the room shook, and were as insensible to all that was going on as logs of wood.

"The time has come!" said Raiko, springing to his feet, and motioning to his men to get to work. One and all hastily opened their knapsacks. Taking out their helmets, their armor, and their long swords, they armed themselves. When they were all ready they all knelt down, and, placing their hands palm to palm, they prayed fervently to their patron gods to help them now in their hour of greatest need and peril.

As they prayed, a shining light filled the room, and in a radiant cloud the three deities appeared again. "Fear not, Warrior Raiko," they said. "We have tied the hands and feet of the demon fast, so you have nothing to fear. While your knights cut off his limbs, do you cut off his head; then kill the rest of the *oni* and your work will be done." The three old men then disappeared as mysteriously as they had come.

Raiko rejoiced at the vision and worshipped with his heart full of gratitude the vanishing deities. The knights then rose from their knees, took their swords and wet the rivets with water, so as to fix the blade firmly in the hilt.

Then they all stole stealthily and cautiously towards Shutendoji. No longer the timid mountain priests; clad in full armor, they were transformed into avenging warriors. With flashing eyes and dauntless mien they moved across the room.

The captive princesses standing round realized that these men were deliverers, from their beloved capital. Their joy and wonder cannot be put into words. Some cried aloud with joy; others covered their faces with their sleeves and burst into soft weeping; others raised their hands to Heaven and exclaimed, "A Buddha come to Hell! Surely these brave men will kill the demons and set us free"; and with clasped hands they entreated the knights to slay their captors and take them back to their homes.

Now Raiko stood over the sleeping Shutendoji with drawn sword, and raising it on high with a mighty sweep he aimed at the demon's neck, which was as big around as a barrel.

The head was severed from the body at one blow, but, horrible to relate, instead of falling to the ground, it flew up into the air in a great rage. It hung over Raiko for a moment snorting flames of fire, and then swooped down as if it would bite off the warrior's head, but it was daunted by the glittering star on his helmet, and drew back and gazed in surprise at the transformed man. Raiko was scorched by the demon's flaming breath. Once more he raised his long sword and striking the terrible head brought it to the ground at last.

The noise of the combat and the triumphant shouts of the warriors awoke the other demons, who roused themselves as quickly as their stupefied senses allowed them. They were in a great fright, and without waiting to get their iron clubs, they made a rush upon Raiko. But they were too late. His five braves dashed in and attacked them right and left, until in a few minutes there was not one left to tell the tale of the destruction which had come down upon them like the autumn whirlwind upon the leaves of the forest glades.

The captive princesses, when they saw that their captors were all slain, jumped about with gladness, waving their long sleeves to and fro, as the tears of joy streamed down their pale faces. They ran to Raiko and caught hold of his sleeves and praised him, saying: "Oh! Raiko Sama, what a brave and noble knight you are! We are indeed grateful to you for having saved our lives. Never have we seen such a wonderful warrior." And with many such expressions of joy they gathered round the knight, and their merry voices were now heard, instead of the groans of the dying cannibals.

Now that Shutendoji was vanquished with all his horde, the way was quite open for Raiko and his men to take the fair captives away from the castle of horror and make their way back to the capital as soon as possible.

First of all Raiko tied up the head of Shutendoji with a strong rope and told the five brave knights to carry it. Then, followed by the princesses, the little band left Mount Oe forever and set out on the homeward journey. When they reached Kyoto the news of Raiko's return spread like fire, and the people came out in crowds to welcome the heroes.

When the parents of the long-lost damsels saw their daughters again, they felt as if they must be dreaming. It seemed too good to be true that the dear and cherished ones should be restored to them safe and well, and they overwhelmed Raiko with praise and with precious gifts.

Raiko took the head of Shutendoji to the Emperor and told him of all that had happened to him. You may be sure that when His Majesty heard of the success which had crowned Raiko and his expedition, he awarded him great praise and merit and bestowed upon him higher Court rank than ever.

In all the country, far and near, Raiko's name was in everyone's mouth, and he was acknowledged to be the greatest warrior in the land. Even in the lonely country places there was not one poor farmer who did not know of the brave deeds of the great general.

Ever since then his portrait is familiar to the children of Japan, for it is often painted on their kites.

Notes

1. Raiko, or Yorimitsu. Both names are written with the same ideographs. Raiko is the Chinese pronunciation, and Yorimitsu the Japanese rendering.
2. Hakama, a divided skirt, part of the Japanese costume.

KIDOMARU THE ROBBER, RAIKO THE BRAVE, AND THE GOBLIN SPIDER

You have just read of the brave knight Raiko's exploits at Oeyama and how he rid the country of the demons who haunted the city of Kyoto and terrified the inhabitants of the Flower Capital (as that city was sometimes called) by their terrible deeds.

There are other interesting stories about him and his fearless warrior-retainers which you may like to hear.

It was not long after Raiko's exploits at Oeyama that the country rang with the name of Kidomaru, a robber and highwayman, who, by his notorious deeds of cruelty and robbery, had caused his name to be feared and hated by all, both young and old.

One evening Raiko with his attendants was returning home from a day's hunting, when he happened to pass the house of his younger brother Yorinobu. The warrior had had a long day out; and having still a good distance to ride before he would reach his own house the thought of a good meal and friendly company, just then, when he was tired and very hungry, was pleasant to contemplate in the lonely hour of twilight. So he called a halt outside the house and sent in word to his brother that he, Raiko, was passing by, and that if Yorinobu had any refreshment to offer his brother, he would call in and stay the night there, as he was tired out on his way back from a day's hunt.

Now in Japan an elder brother or sister commands respect from the younger members of the family, and so Yorinobu was very pleased that Raiko, his elder brother, had condescended to call upon him.

The servant soon returned with the message that Yorinobu was only too pleased to receive Raiko; that he had ordered a feast to be prepared that evening in honor of an unusual event, and as he was alone, nothing could be more opportune or give him greater joy than that his elder brother should have chanced to come by. He humbly begged Raiko that he would deign to share the feast, such as it was, and to pardon the poorness of his hospitality.

Raiko was very pleased with his brother's gracious reception. He quickly flung the reins to his groom, dismounted from his horse, and entered the house, wondering what could be the occasion of Yorinobu's ordering a banquet for himself. When the warrior was shown into the room he found Yorinobu seated on the mats drinking sake, as the servants were bringing in the first dishes of the dinner. When the salutations were over, Yorinobu handed Raiko his wine cup. Raiko took it, and having drained it, asked what his brother meant by the feast he had promised him and what was the occasion of it. Yorinobu laughed as if with triumph, and wheeling round on his cushion pointed out into the garden.

Raiko then looked in the direction indicated by his brother's hand, and saw, tied up to a large pine tree, a young man who could not be much over thirty and of extraordinary strength. The face of the captive expressed hate and ferocity, his body was of an enormous build, while his arms and legs were like trunks of pine trees, so large and brown and muscular were they. His hair was a rough and matted shock, and the eyes glared as if they would start from their sockets. Indeed to Raiko the wild creature looked more like a demon than a human being.

"Well, Yorinobu!" said Raiko, "the occasion of your feast is to say the least unusual; it must certainly have given you some sport to catch that wild creature; but tell me who he is that you have got tied up out there."

"Have you not heard of Kidomaru, the notorious robber?" answered Yorinobu. "There he is! One of my men captured him out on the hills; he found him asleep. The town has long been clamoring for him. He has a big score to settle at last. For tonight I intend to keep him tied up like that, and tomorrow I shall hand him over to the law! Come, let us be merry, for the dinner is served!"

Raiko clapped his hands when he heard of the great feat Yorinobu and his men had accomplished in catching the fearful robber, the terror of whose lawless deeds had long held the people of Kyoto trembling with fear and dread. The outlaw Kidomaru was caught at last and by his own brother Yorinobu! This was an event of rejoicing and congratulation for the family.

"You have certainly done a meritorious service to your country," said he, "but it is ridiculous to tie such a creature up with a rope only. You might just as well think of tying up a wild cow with a fine kite string. It would be less dangerous. Take my advice, Yorinobu, put a strong iron chain round him, or the murderer will soon be at large again."

Yorinobu thought his brother's advice wise, so he clapped his hands. When the servant came to answer the summons, he ordered him to bring an iron chain. When this was brought, he went into the garden, followed by Raiko and his men, and wound it round Kidomaru's body several times, securing it at last to a post with a padlock.

Kidomaru up to this time had rejoiced at his light bonds. He was so strong that he knew he could easily break a rope, and he had waited but for the nightfall to make good his escape under cover of the darkness. You can imagine how great was his anger at Raiko's interference, which was the cause of his being treated with so much severity that his projected escape would now be difficult.

"Hateful man!" muttered Kidomaru to himself. "I will surely punish you for what you have done to me! Remember!" and he threw evil glances at Raiko.

But the brave warrior cared little for the wild robber's malignant glances; he only laughed when he noticed them, and, as the chain was drawn tighter round the robber, he said: "That's right! That chain will hold him sure enough! You must run no risk of his escaping this time!"

Then he and Yorinobu returned to the house, and dinner was served and the two brothers made merry the whole evening, talking over old times, and it was late before they retired to rest.

Now Kidomaru knew that Raiko slept in Yorinobu's house, and he made up his mind to try to slay him that night, for he was mad with wrath at what Raiko had done to him.

"He shall see what I can do!" growled Kidomaru to himself, shaking his rough and shaggy head like a big long-haired terrier. He waited quietly till everyone in the house had gone to rest and all was silent. Then Kidomaru arose, cramped and stiff from sitting tied up so long. With a mighty effort he flung out his great arms, laughing defiance at the chain that bound him. So great was his strength that no second effort was needed; the chain broke and fell clanking to the ground at once, and Kidomaru, like a large hound, shook himself free from his bonds. Softly as a mouse he approached the house and climbed on to the roof, and with one tremendous blow from his huge fist, he broke through the tiles and the boards to the ceiling. His plan was to jump down upon Raiko while he lay sleeping, and taking him unawares suddenly to cut off his head. But the warrior had lain down to rest expecting such an attack, and he had slept but lightly. As soon as he heard the noise above him, he was wide awake in an instant, and to warn his enemy he coughed and cleared his throat. Kidomaru was a man of fierce and dauntless character, and he was not in the least thrown back in his purpose by finding that Raiko was awake. He went on with his work of making a hole large enough in the ceiling to let himself through to the room beneath.

Raiko now sat up and clapped his hands loudly to summon his men, who slept in an adjoining room. Watanabe, the chief man-at-arms, came out to see what his master wanted.

"Watanabe," said Raiko, "my sleep has been disturbed by something moving in the ceiling. It may be a weasel, for weasels are noisy creatures. It cannot be a rat, for a rat is not large enough to make so much noise. At any rate, it seems impossible to sleep tonight, so saddle the horses and get all the men ready to start. I will get up and ride out to the Temple of Mount Kurama. I want all the men to accompany me."

Perched between the roof and the ceiling, the robber heard all this, and said to himself: "What ho! Raiko goes to Kurama! That is good news! Instead of wasting my time here like a rat in a trap, I will set out for Kurama immediately and get there before those stupid men can, and I will waylay them and kill them all." So Kidomaru crawled out on the roof again, let himself down to the ground, and hurried with all the speed he could make to Kurama.

A large plain had to be crossed in going from the city to Kurama, and here a number of wild cattle had their home. When Kidomaru, on his way to Kurama, came to this spot, a plan flashed across his mind by which he could steal a march on Raiko. He soon caught one of the big oxen a blow on the head. Three blows one after the other, and the ox fell dead at the robber's feet. Kidomaru then proceeded to strip off its skin. It was very hard work, but he managed to do it quickly, so strong was he, and then throwing the hide over himself he lay down completely disguised, a man in a bull's hide, and waited for Raiko and his men to come.

He had not long to wait. Raiko, followed by his four braves, soon came in sight. The warrior reined in his horse when he came to the plain and saw the cattle. He turned to his men and said: "Here is a place where we may find some sport. Instead of going on to Kurama, let us stay here and have some hunting! Look at the wild cattle!"

The four retainers with one accord all gladly agreed to their chief's proposal, for they loved sport and adventure just as much as Raiko and were glad of an excuse to show their skill as huntsmen. The sun was just rising, and the prospect of a fine morning added zest to the pastime. Each man prepared his bow and arrows in readiness to begin the chase.

But the cattle, thus disturbed, did not enjoy the sport. Man's play was their death indeed. One of their number had been killed by Kidomaru, and now they were attacked by Raiko and his men, who came riding furiously into their midst, shooting at them with bows and arrows. With angry snorts, whisking their tails on high and butting with their horns, they ran to right and left. In the general stampede that followed their attack, the hunters noticed that one animal lay still in the tall grass. At first they thought it must be either lame or ill, so they took no notice of it, and left it alone till Raiko came riding up. He went up and looked at it carefully, and then ordered one of his men to shoot it.

The man obeyed, and taking his bow, shot an arrow at the recumbent animal. The arrow did not hit the mark; for, to the astonishment of the four hunters, the hide was flung aside and out stepped the robber Kidomaru.

"You, Raiko! It is you, is it?" exclaimed he. "Do you know that I have a spite against you?" and with these words he darted forward and attacked Raiko with a dagger. But Raiko did not even move in his saddle. He drew his sword and, adroitly guarding himself, exchanged two or three strokes with the robber, and then slashed off his head. But wonderful to relate, so strong was the will that animated Kidomaru that though his head was cut off, his body stood up straight and firm till his right arm, still holding the dagger, struck at Raiko's saddle. Then, and not till then, it collapsed. It is said that the warriors were all greatly impressed by the malevolent spirit of the robber, which was strong enough to stir the body to action even after the head had been severed from the shoulders.

Such was the death of the notorious robber Kidomaru, at the hands of the brave warrior Raiko who was awarded much praise for the clever way in which he drew Kidomaru out as far as Kurama to kill him. He had understood from Kidomaru's evil glances that the robber planned to kill him, and he thus avoided causing trouble in his brother's house. In this instance, as always, Raiko displayed wisdom and bravery.

No sooner, however, was Kidomaru killed, than news was brought to the capital that another man had arisen who imitated Kidomaru in his daily deeds of robbery and other wicked acts. This robber's name was Kakamadare.

One bright moonlight night, Kakamadare was waiting on the plain between Kyoto and Kurama for travelers to come that way, hoping that luck would bring some rich man into his clutches. Presently he heard someone coming towards him playing on a flute. Thinking this somewhat strange, he hid himself in the grass and waited to see who would appear. The sweet music drew nearer and nearer, and then the player came in view. The light of the moon made everything as clear as day, and the robber saw a handsome samurai of soldierly aspect, dressed in beautiful silken robes and wearing a long sword at his side.

"Now's my opportunity; I'm in luck tonight," thought the robber, as he rose from his hiding place and stealthily followed the flute player. As he kept step by step behind him, Kakamadare drew his sword in readiness several times to cut down his prey, and waited for the chance to strike.

All at once the samurai turned and looked steadily at the robber, who began to tremble. Then the knight calmly and coolly resumed his playing, as if utterly indifferent to the danger which threatened him. Once more the robber followed, with the intention of cutting the man down, but the opportunity for which he waited never came; each time his hand went up with his sword, it as quickly fell to his side. A spirit of high and noble purpose seemed to emanate from the knight, which cowed the man behind and made him weak. For so great is the virtue of the sword that in Japan it is an acknowledged fact that all noble swordsmen had this power of subduing lesser natures by the spiritual grace which went forth from them. Indeed the belief in the occult power of the sword was great, and it was said that no bad man could keep the possession of a fine blade.

Kakamadare could not strike. He could not tell the cause of his weakness. He thought that it might be the influence of the music. He found himself listening to the gentle strains of the flute, and admiring the skill with which the man played. He noticed the firm and fearless air of the knight as he walked and his great nerve. The man knew himself to be followed by a robber, yet he showed not the least concern. Kakamadare tried to turn back now, but he found that he could do nothing but follow the man in front of him. In this way the strange pair reached the town. Kakamadare now made a great effort to break the spell, and was on the point of turning back and trying to escape from the strange, compelling presence, when to his astonishment the samurai suddenly wheeled round upon him and said: "Kakamadare, I thank you for your trouble! You have given me a safe escort!"

At this the robber became so terrified that he fell down on his knees and was unable to move or speak for some moments. At last, so soon as his tongue found utterance, he said: "I know not who you are, but I beg you to forgive me! I would have killed you!"

He then confessed everything to the knight. He told him of his many deeds of robbery and violence which had made him feared and hated by the people, who thought that he must be a demon, for so cruel and relentless was he that he never showed mercy even to the poorest peasant. "I have never met anyone like you," Kakamadare went on to say. "I promise to give up my life as a robber, and I beg you to take me into your service as one of the humblest of your retainers."

The knight led the man home, and gave him some good clothes, telling him that when he again got into straits and wanted money or clothes, he might come a second time to the house, but that it was unwise to show such contempt for others as to enter into an encounter where he himself might be the injured party.

This kindness and mercy touched the man's heart, and from that day he became a reformed man and a law-abiding citizen.

The knight was none other than Hirai, one of the warriors who accompanied Raiko in his successful expedition against the demons of Oeyama. There is a saying that "Brave generals make brave soldiers," and it is quite true. Raiko was a man of great sagacity and courage, and his band of braves and the knight Hirai, of whom we have just read, were like their master. There were no men in the whole of Japan braver than they. This proves the truth of the old adage.

There is another story about the General Raiko which you may like to hear. The sword with which Raiko slew Kidomaru was called the Kumokiri, or Spider-Cutting Sword, and about the naming of this blade there is an interesting story.

It happened at one time that Raiko was unwell and was obliged to keep his room. Every night at about twelve a little acolyte would come to his bedside, and in a kind and gentle way pour out and give him some medicine to take. Raiko noticed that he did not know the boy, but as there were many under-lings in the servants' quarters whom he never saw, this did not strike him as strange. But Raiko, instead of recovering, found himself growing weaker and weaker, and especially after taking the medicine he always felt worse.

At last one day he spoke to his head servant and asked him who it was that brought him medicine every night, but the attendant answered that he knew nothing about the medicine and that there was no acolyte in the house.

Raiko now suspected some supernatural snare. "Some malevolent being is taking advantage of my illness and trying to bewitch me or to cause my death. When the boy comes again tonight I will find out his real form. He may be a fox or goblin in disguise!" said Raiko.

So he waited for the appearance of the acolyte, wondering what the strange incident could mean.

When midnight came, the boy, as usual, appeared, bringing with him the usual cup of medicine. The knight calmly took the cup from the boy and said, "Thank you for your trouble!" but instead of swallowing the false medicine, he threw it, cup and all, at the boy's head. Then jumping up he seized the sword that lay beside his bed and cut at the impostor. As the blade fell, the acolyte screamed with rage and pain, then, with a movement as quick as lightning, before he turned to escape from the room, he threw something at the knight, which, marvelous to relate, as he threw, spread outwards pyramidically into a large white sticky web which fell over Raiko and clung to him so that he could hardly move. Raiko whirled his sword round and cut the clinging meshes and freed himself; again the goblin threw a web over him, and again Raiko cut the enmeshing threads away; once more the huge spider's web—for such it was—was thrown over him, and then the goblin fled. Raiko called for his men and then sank exhausted on his bed.

His chief retainer, answering the summons, met the acolyte in the corridor, and thinking it strange that an unknown priest, however young, should come from his master's room at that hour of the night, stopped him with drawn sword.

The goblin answered not a word, but threw his entangling web over the man and mysteriously disappeared.

Now thoroughly alarmed, the retainer hastened to Raiko. Great was his consternation when he saw his master, with the meshes of the goblin's web still clinging to him.

"See!" exclaimed Raiko, pointing to the threads still clinging to his man and himself, "a goblin spider has been here!"

He then gave orders to hunt down the goblin, but the thing could nowhere be found. On the white mats and along the corridors they found as they searched red drops of blood, which showed that the creature had been wounded.

Raiko's men followed the red trail, out into the garden, across the city to the hills, till they came to a cave, and here the blood drops ceased. Groans and cries of pain issued from the cave, so the warriors felt sure that they had come to the end of their hunt.

"The goblin is surely hiding in that cave!" they all said. Drawing their swords, they entered the cave and found a monster spider writhing with pain and bleeding from a deep sword cut on the head. They at once killed the creature and carried it to Raiko.

The knight had often heard stories of these dreadful spiders, but had never seen one before.

"It was this goblin spider then that wanted to prey upon me! The net that was thrown over me was a spider's web! Of all my adventures this is the strangest!" said Raiko.

That night Raiko ordered a banquet to be prepared for all his retainers in honor of the event, and he drank to the health of his five brave men.

From that time the acolyte never appeared and Raiko recovered his health and strength at once.

Such is the story of the Kumokiri Sword. *Kumo* means "spider," and *kiri* means "cutting," and it was so named because it cut to death the goblin spider who haunted the brave knight Raiko.

A Cherry Flower Idyll

About one hundred years ago, in the old capital of Kyoto, there lived a young man named Taira Shunko. At the time this story opens he was about twenty years of age, of prepossessing appearance, amiable disposition, and refined tastes, his favorite pastime being the composition of poetry. His father decided that Shunko should finish his education in Edo, the Eastern capital, where he was accordingly sent. He proved himself an apt scholar, more clever than his fellow students, which won him the favor of the tutor in whose charge he had been placed.

Some months after his arrival in Edo, he went to stay at his uncle's house during convalescence from a slight illness. By the time he was well again the spring had come, and the call of the cherry flower season found a ready response in Shunko's heart, so he determined to visit Koganei, a place famous for its cherry trees.

One fine morning he arose at dawn, and, equipped with a small luncheon box and a gourd filled with sake, set out on his way.

In the good old days, as now, Koganei was celebrated for the beauty of its scenery in the springtime. Thousands of spreading trees formed a glorious avenue on either side of the blue waters of the River Tama, and when these burst into clouds of diaphanous bloom, visitors from far and near came in crowds to join in the revel of the Queen of Flowers. Beneath the shade of the over-arching trees, teahouses were dotted along the banks of the stream. Here, with the shoji hospitably open on all sides, tempting meals of river trout, bamboo shoots, and fern curls, and sundry and manifold dainties were served to the pleasure-seeking traveller.

Shunko rested at one of these riverside hostelries, refreshing himself with generous draughts from his gourd, and then opened his tiny luncheon box, the contents of which he supplemented with the delicate river trout, fresh from the pellucid waters of the stream and artistically prepared by the teahouse cuisine.

Under the influence of wine, the homesickness which had been oppressing his soul gradually took wings; he became merry, and felt as if he were at home in his own beautiful city of Kyoto. He sauntered along under the trees, singing snatches of songs in praise of this favorite flower. On every side the whole world was framed in softest clouds of ethereal bloom, which seemed to waft him along between earth and heaven.

Lost in admiration at the fairylike beauty of the scene, he wandered on and on, oblivious of time, till he suddenly realized that daylight was on the wane. A zephyr sprang up, scattering the petals of the blossoms like a fall of scented snow, and as Shunko gazed around, he became aware that the last visitors had gone, and that he was left alone with only the birds twittering on their way to their nests to remind him that he, too, like the rest of belated humanity, ought to be wending his way home.

However, sinking down upon a mossy bank beneath a cherry tree, he became lost in meditation. With the aid of a portable ink box and brush he composed some stanzas, a rhapsody on the transcendent loveliness of the cherry flowers.

Song to the Spirit of the Cherry Blossom[1]
Throughout the land the Spring doth hold high Court,
Obedient to the call from far I come
To lay my tribute at thy matchless shrine,
To vow allegiance to the Queen of Flowers.

How can I praise aright thy perfume sweet,
The heavenly pureness of thy blossom's snow:
Spellbound I linger in thy Kingdom fair
That rivets me, love's prisoner!

Take this poor bud of poesy to thy fragrant breast,
There let it hang, symbol of homage true:
Ne'er can perfection be acclaimed right,
Much less thy beauties, which are infinite!
Thy by fragile petals fluttering on my robes
Pluck at my heart, and bind me to thy realm.
With fairy fetters—ne'er can I leave thy bowers
But worship thee forevermore, my peerless Queen of Flowers!

Having tied the slip of paper to a branch of the tree in whose shade he had been reclining, he turned to retrace his steps, but realized, with a start, that the twilight had merged into darkness, and the pale gleams of the crescent moon were already beginning to illumine the deep blue vault above him. During his abstraction he had wandered off the beaten track, and was following a totally unknown path which grew more and more intricate among the hills. It had been a long day, and he was growing faint with hunger and weary from fatigue when, just as he was beginning to despair of ever finding an escape from such a labyrinth, suddenly a young girl appeared from the gloom as if by magic! By the fitful light of the lantern she was carrying, Shunko saw that she was very fair and dainty, and concluded that she was in the service of some household of rank. To his surprise she took his presence as a matter of course, and politely addressed him, with many bows:

"My mistress is awaiting you. Please come and I will show you the way."

Shunko was still more astonished at these words. He had never been in this wild and unknown place before, and could not imagine what human soul could know and summon him thus, at this late hour.

After a few moments' silence he inquired of the little messenger, "Who is your mistress?"

"You will understand when you see her," she replied. "My lady told me that as you had lost your way, I was to come and guide you to her house, so kindly follow me without delay."

Shunko's perplexity was only increased by these words, but after reflection, he told himself that probably one of his friends must be living in Koganei without his knowledge, and he decided to follow the fair messenger without further questioning.

Setting out at a swift pace, she guided him into a small valley, through which a mountain stream was murmuring in its rocky bed. It was a remote and sheltered spot. Presently a turn in the path led them to a tiny dwelling, completely surrounded and overshadowed by a cluster of cherry trees in full bloom. The girl stopped before the little bamboo gate. Shunko hesitated, but she turned to him with a smile.

"This is the house where my mistress dwells. Be so good as to enter!"

Shunko obeyed, and passed up a miniature garden to the entrance. Another little maiden appeared with a lighted candle, and ushered Shunko through several anterooms leading to a large guest chamber, which seemed to be overhanging the crystal waters of a lake, in whose depth, like golden flowers, he could see the reflection of myriad stars. He noticed that the appointments were all of a most sumptuous description. Cherry blossoms formed the keynote of the decorations; the screens were all planted with the flowering branches, clusters of them adorned the *tokonoma*; while the high-standing candlesticks were of massive silver, as were also the charcoal braziers, the glow of which drove out the chill of the spring evening. Beautiful crepe cushions were placed beside the braziers, as if in expectation of a welcome guest; while the perfume of rare incense, mingling with the delicious fragrance of cherry blossom, floated through the room.

Shunko was too bewildered and too exhausted by his long wanderings to indulge in reflections. With the unreal sensations of an errant hero of a fairy tale, he sank upon the mats and waited, wondering what would happen next.

Suddenly, the rustle of silken garments arrested his attention; noiselessly the screens of the room slid back, and the apparition of a beautiful maiden appeared, exquisitely graceful in her trailing robes.

She was in the prime of youth, and could not have been more than seventeen years of age. Her dress, in which the skies of spring seemed to be reflected, was the hue of a rich azure blue, and the crepe fabric was half concealed beneath sprays of cherry bloom so deftly worked, and with such a moonlit sheen upon them, that Shunko thought that they must have been woven from the moonbeams of the serene far-off moon for the Goddess of Spring. Her face was so perfect that the wondering guest was speechless at the loveliness of the vision before him. Never had he dreamed of such beauty, although he came from Kyoto, the city of beautiful women.

The fair hostess, noting his embarrassment, laughed softly, as she took her seat beside one of the silver braziers, and with a gentle gesture of the hand assigned him the companion place opposite her.

Bowing to the ground, she said:

"Ever have I lived alone in this place with only the river and the hills for my friends. So that your coming is a great joy and consolation to me. It is my wish to prepare a feast of welcome for you, but alas! in the depths of the woods, there is nothing meet for an honored guest, but, poor as our entertainment is, I beg you, not to despise it."

A servant then appeared bearing trays of delicious dishes, with a golden wine flagon and a crystal cup.

At the sound of her voice, enchantment seemed to weave a subtle net around the bewildered Shunko; a languorous feeling of delight stole over his senses, and he yielded himself to the mysterious charm of the hour.

His lovely hostess proffered to her guest the crystal wine cup, and filled it to the brim with amber wine from the golden flask.

As Shunko quaffed it, he thought never had such delicious nectar been tasted by mortal man. He could not resist cup after cup, till gradually all apprehension of the unknown surroundings passed away, and a strange gladness filled his heart as he succumbed to the charm of the hour, while servants silently went to and fro bearing fresh and tempting dainties to lay before him.

While they were conversing happily together the lady left his side, and seating herself beside the koto, began to sing a wild and beautiful air. Strange and wonderful to relate, the song was none other than the self-same poem which Shunko had composed that very evening, and had left fluttering from the branch of the cherry tree beneath whose canopy of bloom he had rested. Falling completely under the bewitchment of his surroundings, Shunko felt that he wished to stay there for evermore, and a pang smote his breast at the thought that he soon must separate, if only for a few hours, from his mystic lady of the vale of cherry blossoms.

As the last plaintive chord throbbed into silence, a chime in the next room struck two in the morning.

Laying the instrument aside, she said:

"At this late hour it is impossible for you to return home tonight. Everything is prepared in the next room. Honorably deign to rest. Forgive me that I cannot entertain you in a more befitting manner, in this, our poor home."

Attendants then entering, the screens were drawn aside for their guest, and he passed into the adjoining chamber, which had been prepared as a sleeping apartment. Sinking to rest among the silken coverlets and luxurious quilts, he was soon lost in heavy slumber.

Suddenly, in the morning, he was awakened by a cold wind blowing across his face. Day had broken, and the rosy dawn was flushing the horizon in the east. Slowly returning to his senses, he found himself lying on the ground beneath the very cherry tree that had inspired his poem of the day before; but his wonderful adventure, his charming hostess, and her waiting maidens were no more! Shunko, lost in wonder, recalled over and over again the glowing memories of the preceding evening, but the vision had been so vivid that he felt assured it must have been something more than the mere phantoms of a dream. An overpowering conviction crept over him that the lovely maiden had her living counterpart in this world of realities.

From his earliest childhood he had always offered a special devotion to the cherry flowers. Year after year, in the springtime, he had taken special joy in visiting some place noted for their blossoms. Could it be that the spirit of the cherry tree, to whose beauty he had dedicated his poem, had appeared to him in human form to reward him for his lifelong fidelity?

At last he rose and stretched his cramped limbs, and musing only on the vanished wonders of the night, wandered aimlessly along. At length he regained the main road and slowly turned his errant footsteps towards home.

Although he took up his usual life again, he could not forget his experiences in the cherry blossom valley, they haunted him not only in the silent watches of the night, but in the bright noontide of day. Three days later he returned to Koganei, with the fond hope of evoking once again the longed-for vision of the lovely girl who had so bewitched him with her beauty and her charm.

But, alas for human hopes! In those short days all had changed. What so ephemeral as the reign of the cherry flower in the spring! Gray were the skies that had been so blue and fair; bleak and deserted was the scene that had been so gay and full of life; bare of blossom, and stripped of their fairy beauty were the trees, whose petals of blushing snow the relentless wind had scattered far and wide.

As before, he rested at the same little teahouse by the river and waited for the shades of evening to fall. Roaming about in the deepening twilight, he anxiously sought some sign or token, but vain were all his efforts to find the valley of dream again. Vanished was the little dwelling in the shadow of the cherry groves. Nowhere by unfamiliar paths could he find the fair messenger who had guided him to the bamboo gate. All had faded and suffered change.

Year after year, in the springtime, did Shunko make a pilgrimage of loving memory to the same spot, but though his faithfulness was never rewarded by a sight of her, who had so completely taken possession of his heart and soul, yet the flower of hope never faded, and firm was his resolution, that none other than the maiden of Koganei should ever be his wife.

About five years passed. Then a sudden summons from his home arrived, bearing the sorrowful tidings that his father had been stricken with severe illness, and begging him to return without delay.

That very day he made all arrangements, and disposed of his few student's belongings in readiness to set out at daybreak.

It happened to be the season of autumn when, in the Orient, the deer cries for its mate in the flaming maple glades of the forest, and a young man's heart[2] is filled with what the Japanese call *mono no aware wo shiru* ("the Ah-ness of things").

Shunko was sad. He yearned for the lovely girl who had so bewitched him, and in addition to this sorrow his heart was heavy at the thought of his father's illness.

As Shunko proceeded on his journey his depression increased, and sadly he repeated aloud the following lines:

> *Cold as the wind of early spring*
> *Chilling the buds that still lie sheathed*
> *In their brown armor with its sting,*
> *And the bare branches withering—*
> *So seems the human heart to me!*

Cold as the March wind's bitterness;
I am alone, none comes to see
Or cheer me in these days of stress.

Now it chanced that an old man heard this mournful recital, and took pity on Shunko.

"Pray pardon a stranger intruding upon your privacy," said the old man, "but we sometimes take a gloomy view of life for want of good cheer. It may be that you have traveled far and are footsore and weary. If that is so, be honorably pleased to accept rest and refreshment in my humble house in yonder valley."

Shunko was pleased with the old man's kindly manner, and warmly accepted his hospitality.

After a hearty meal and a long chat with the old man, Shunko retired to bed.

The youth had no sooner closed his eyes than he found himself dreaming of Koganei and of the beautiful woman he had met there. A gentle breeze was full of the scent of flowers. He noticed a cloud of cherry blossom falling like a little company of white butterflies to the ground. While watching so pleasing a scene he observed a strip of paper hanging to one of the lower branches. He advanced close to the tree to discover that someone had written a poem on the wind-blown paper.

A thrill passed through him as he read the words:

Lingers still the past within thy memory?
East of the Temple let thy footsteps stray
And there await thy destiny!

Earnestly he repeated the lines over and over again, and awoke to find himself still reciting the little verse that seemed so full of meaning. Deeply he pondered over his dream. How could he solve the enigmatic message it surely bore for him? What did it portend?

The next day he set out on his journey to the west. His father was in the last stages of his malady, and the doctors had given up all hope of his recovery. In a few weeks the old man died, and Shunko succeeded to the estate. It was a sad winter, and the young man with his widowed mother were secluded in the house for some months, observing the strictest retirement during the period of mourning.

But youth soon recovers from its griefs, and by the time that April had come with the dear beguilement of her blue skies and flowering landscapes, Shunko, in company with an old friend, set out to assuage his sorrows in the viewing of his favorite cherry trees, and to find balm for his soul in the golden sunshine of spring. His father's death, and the business of attending to the affairs of succession, had left him but little leisure for vain regrets, and the family upheaval he had experienced the last few months had somewhat dimmed the memory of the mysterious dream, which had come to him the night before his return home.

But now, with a strange and eerie sensation, he realized that, unwittingly, Fate had guided their footsteps to the Eastern Mountain, and that the way they had chosen was *East of the Temple* Chionin. The message on the scroll flashed into his mind as he sauntered along:

Lingers still the past within thy memory?
East of the Temple let thy footsteps stray,
And there await thy destiny!

By this time they had reached the famous avenue of cherry trees, and the pearly mist of bloom, that seemed to envelope them like a fragrant cloud, at once recalled to Shunko's mind how striking was the resemblance this fairy-like spot bore to Koganei.

Just at that moment he espied a small glittering object lying on the ground at the root of one of the cherry trees. It proved to be a golden ring, and engraven on it was the hieroglyphic "Hana," which may be interpreted as meaning either "Flower" or "Cherry Blossom."

As the afternoon began to wane they came to a teahouse, which seemed to look especially inviting, and here they rested and refreshed their weariness as the shadows gradually lengthened into the twilight.

In the next room were two or three girls' voices talking gaily together, and their laughter sounded soft and musical as it floated out into the balmy air of that soft evening of spring.

By degrees Shunko found himself overhearing snatches of their conversation, and at length he distinctly caught the words:

"The day has been a perfect one except for one little cloud. O Hana San's ring...."

Then a silvery voice made answer: "The mere loss of the ring is nothing, but as it bears my name, it grieves me that it should fall into the hands of a stranger."

At these words Shunko impetuously rose and entered the adjoining chamber.

"Pardon me," he cried, "but can this be the lost ring?" and he held out to the little group the trinket which he had found beneath the cherry tree that afternoon.

The youngest of the trio, a graceful girl of about seventeen or eighteen summers, bowed to the ground, murmuring her thanks, while an elderly woman, who was evidently her foster nurse, came forward to receive the missing treasure.

As the young girl raised her head, Shunko felt a thrilling shock of recognition quiver through his frame. At last the gods had granted his fervent prayers. Before him, as a living and breathing reality, he beheld the long sought maiden of the vision at Koganei. The room, its occupants, and all around him faded away, and his soul was wafted back through the vista of years to the lonely valley of dreams, so far away.

This, then, was the significance of the mystic writing in the deserted house, that now he had served his term of probation and was at last deemed worthy of the beloved one for whom he had waited and longed for so many years.

The elderly nurse was aware of his embarrassment, and tactfully attempted to come to his aid. She proffered wine and refreshments, and made several inquiries as to where he had found the ring and where he lived.

After replying to these queries, Shunko, who was in no mood for talking, withdrew with deep obeisances, and slowly wended his way homewards, lost in abstraction.

Oh, the delight of it! To be alone with his reverie and thoughts of her, whom he had scarcely hoped to see again, the lady of his dreams! Both head and heart were in a whirl. And the wonder of his adventure kept him awake through the midnight darkness. Only at the break of dawn did he fall into a troubled sleep.

Towards noon his belated slumbers were disturbed by a servant, who came to announce the advent of a visitor, who urgently desired an interview. He arose in haste, and there awaiting him in the guest room was the foster nurse of the day before. Rich gifts of silk lay on the mats, and with the explanation that she had been sent by the parents of her young charge, she came to express their thanks for the incident of the day before.

When the formalities of greeting were exchanged, Shunko could no longer keep silence regarding the subject nearest his heart, and begged the nurse to tell him, in confidence, all she could concerning O Hana San.

"My young mistress belongs to a knightly family. There are three children in all, but she is the only girl, and the youngest child. She is just seventeen years of age, and is quite renowned for her beauty, which, as you have seen her, you may perhaps understand. Many have ardently desired her hand in marriage, but hitherto all have been declined. She cares nothing for worldly things and devotes herself to study."

"Why does she refuse to marry?" asked the young man, with a beating heart.

"Ah! there is a strange reason for that!" replied the nurse, and her voice dropped to a whisper. "Several years ago, when she was not much more than a child, her mother and I took her to visit the beautiful Kiyomizu Temple in the springtime to see the cherry flowers. As you know, Kwannon, the Goddess of Mercy of that temple, takes under her protection all lovers who pray to her for a happy union, and the railings round her shrine are white with the tying of paper-prayer love knots innumerable. O Hana's mother told me afterwards that when we passed before Kwannon's altar, she had offered up a special prayer for her daughter's future happiness in marriage.

"While we were walking in the vicinity of the waterfall below the temple, we suddenly lost sight of Hana for a few minutes. It seems that, wrapt in wonder at the beauty of the blossoming trees, she had strayed away, and was listening to the foaming water as it dashed over the boulders of rock. Suddenly, a gust of wind blew over us. It was icy cold! We looked round for O Hana San, and you can imagine the fear that seized our hearts when we found that she had disappeared. In a frenzy of anxiety I ran hither and thither, and at last caught sight of her prostrate on the ground at some distance away. She had fallen into a deep faint near the cascade, and was lying there pale and senseless, and drenched with spray. We carried her to the nearest teahouse, and tried every means in our power to restore her to consciousness, but she remained sunk in a deep swoon all through that long, long day. Her mother wept, fearing that she was dead. When the sun set and no change took place, we were lost in the anguish of despair. All of a sudden an old priest appeared before us. Staff in hand, and clad in ancient and dilapidated garments, he seemed an apparition from some past and bygone age. He gazed long at the senseless girl, lying white and cold in the semblance of death, and then sank on his knees by her side, absorbed in silent prayer, now and again gently stroking her inanimate body with his rosary.

"All through the night we watched thus by O Hana San, and never did hours seem so interminable or so black. At last, towards the dawn, success crowned the old man's efforts; the spell that had so mysteriously changed her youth and bloom into a pallid mask, was gradually exorcised, her spirit returned, and with a gentle sigh, O Hana San was restored to life.

"Her mother was transported with joy. When she was able to speak, she murmured, 'Praise be to the mercy of the holy Kwannon of Kiyomizu!' and again and again she expressed her fervent gratitude to the queer priest.

"In answer he took from the folds of his robe a poem-card, which he handed to my mistress.

"'This,' said he, 'was written by your daughter's future bridegroom. In a few years he will come to claim her, therefore keep this poem as the token.'

"With these words he disappeared as unexpectedly and mysteriously as he had come. Great was our desire to know more of the meaning of those fateful words, but though we made inquiries of everyone in the temple grounds, not a soul had seen a trace of the ancient priest. O Hana San seemed none the worse for her long swoon, and we returned home, marveling greatly at the extraordinary events that had happened to us that day and night in the temple of Kiyomizu.

"From that time onwards I noticed a great change in O Hana San. She was no longer a child. Though only thirteen years of age, she grew serious and thoughtful, and studied her books with great diligence. In music she especially excelled, and all were astonished at her great talent. As she grew in years, her amiability and charm became quite noted in the neighborhood: her mother realizes that she is at the zenith of her youth and beauty, and, many a time, has tried to find the author of the poem, but hitherto her efforts have been of no avail.

"Yesterday we had the good fortune to meet you, and if you will forgive my boldness, it seemed to me as though Fate had especially directed you to my foster child. On our return home, we related all that had befallen us to my mistress. She listened to our recital with deep agitation, and then exclaimed, with joy: 'Thanks be to Heaven! At last the long-sought-for one has come!'"

Shunko felt as if in a trance. Full well he knew that the Gods had guided his footsteps to their yearned-for goal, and the maiden to whom he had restored the little golden circlet, was none other than the one for whom his heart had hungered for many years.

It was, indeed, a supreme Fate that had linked their lives in one.

In taking farewell of the old nurse, Shunko entrusted to her his message to his bride-elect—the mysterious token of affinity composed beneath the cherry tree five years ago.

There was no longer any doubt but that O Hana's destiny was indeed fulfilled. The bridegroom, foretold by the age-old priest, had come at last. Her mother's prayer offered up at the temple of the Kwannon of Kiyomizu had been heard. Both parents rejoiced at the happy fate that the Powers above had vouchsafed to their beloved child, an eminent soothsayer was consulted, and a specially auspicious day was chosen for the wedding.

When the excitement of the bridal feast was over and Shunko was left alone with his lovely bride, he noticed that her wedding robe of turquoise blue, scattered over with embroideries of her name-flower, was the selfsame one that had been worn by his visionary hostess; and, moreover, comparisons proved that the date of her long trance at Kiyomizu was identical with that of his prophetic vision at Koganei.

A great gladness filled the bridegroom's heart, for he felt that in some mystical way his bride and dream-love were one and the same incarnate. The spirit of the cherry tree had surely entered into Hana when she had lost consciousness at the Kiyomizu temple, and En-musubi no Kami, the God of Marriage, had assumed the disguise of the old priest, and with the magnetic threads of love, had woven their destinies together.

And Shunko tenderly caressed his bride, saying:

"I have known and loved and waited for you ever since your spirit came to me from the Kiyomizu temple."

And he told her all that had befallen him at Koganei.

The young lovers thereupon pledged their love to each other for many lives to come, and lived blissfully to the end of their days.

Notes
1. The verse in this story was translated by Countess Iso-ko-Mutsu.
2. At this point there is a break in Ozaki's manuscript, and the gap has been filled up by another hand. Ozaki resumes her story with "A thrill passed through him...".

URASHIMA

Urashima was a fisherman of the Inland Sea. Every night he plied his trade. He caught fishes both great and small, being upon the sea through the long hours of darkness. Thus he made his living.

Upon a certain night the moon shone brightly, making plain the paths of the sea. And Urashima kneeled in his boat and dabbled his right hand in the green water. Low he leaned, till his hair lay spread upon the waves, and he paid no heed to his boat that listed or to his trailing fish net. He drifted in his boat till he came to a haunted place. And he was neither waking nor sleeping, for the moon made him mad.

Then the Daughter of the Deep Sea arose, and she took the fisherman in her arms, and sank with him, down, down, to her cold sea cave. She laid him upon a sandy bed, and long did she look upon him. She cast her sea spell upon him, and sang her sea songs to him and held his eyes with hers.

He said, "Who are you, lady?"

She told him, "The Daughter of the Deep Sea."

"Let me go home," he said. "My little children wait and are tired."
"Nay, rather stay with me," she said:

> "Urashima,
> Thou Fisherman of the Inland Sea,
> Thou art beautiful;
> Thy long hair is twisted round my heart;
> Go not from me.
> Only forget thy home."

"Ah, now," said the fisherman, "let be, for the dear gods' sake. I would go to mine own." But she said again:

> "Urashima,
> Thou Fisherman of the Inland Sea,
> I'll set thy couch with pearl;
> I'll spread thy couch with seaweed and sea flowers;
> Thou shalt be King of the Deep Sea,
> And we will reign together"

"Let me go home," said Urashima. "My little children wait and are tired." But she said:

> "Urashima,
> Thou Fisherman of the Inland Sea,
> Never be afraid of the Deep Sea tempest;
> We will roll rocks about our cavern doors;
> Neither be afraid of the drowned dead;
> Thou shalt not die."

"Ah, now," said the fisherman, "let be, for the dear gods' sake. I would go to mine own."
"Stay with me this one night."
"Nay, not one."
Then the Daughter of the Deep Sea wept, and Urashima saw her tears.

"I will stay with you this one night," he said.

So after the night was passed, she brought him up to the sand and the seashore.

"Are we near your home?" she said.

He told her, "Within a stone's throw."

"Take this," she said, "in memory of me." She gave him a casket of mother-of-pearl; it was rainbow-tinted and its clasps were of coral and of jade.

"Do not open it," she said. "O fisherman, do not open it." And with that she sank and was no more seen, the Daughter of the Deep Sea.

As for Urashima, he ran beneath the pine trees to come to his dear home. And as he went he laughed for joy. And he tossed up the casket to catch the sun.

"Ah, me," he said, "the sweet scent of the pines!" So he went calling to his children with a call that he had taught them, like a seabird's note. Soon he said, "Are they yet asleep ? It is strange they do not answer me."

Now when he came to his house he found four lonely walls, moss-grown. Nightshade flourished on the threshold, death lilies by the hearth, dianthus and lady fern. No living soul was there.

"Now what is this?" cried Urashima. "Have I lost my wits? Have I left my eyes in the deep sea?"

He sat down upon the grassy floor and thought long. "The dear gods help me!" he said. "Where is my wife, and where are my little children?"

He went to the village, where he knew the stones in the way, and every tiled and tilted eave was to him most familiar; and here he found folk walking to and fro, going upon their business. But they were all strange to him.

"Good morrow," they said, "good morrow, wayfarer. Do you tarry in our town?"

He saw children at their play, and often he put his hand beneath their chins to turn their faces up. Alas! he did it all in vain.

"Where are my little children," he said, "O Lady Kwannon the Merciful? Peradventure the gods know the meaning of all this; it is too much for me."

When sunset came, his heart was heavy as stone, and he went and stood at the parting of the ways outside the town. As men passed by he pulled them by the sleeve:

"Friend," he said, "I ask your pardon, did you know a fisherman of this place called Urashima?"

And the men that passed by answered him, "We never heard of such an one."

There passed by the peasant people from the mountains. Some went afoot, some rode on patient packhorses. They went singing their country songs, and they carried baskets of wild strawberries or sheaves of lilies bound upon their backs. And the lilies nodded as they went. Pilgrims passed by, all clad in white, with staves and rice-straw hats, sandals fast bound and gourds of water. Swiftly they went, softly they went, thinking of holy things. And lords and ladies passed by, in brave attire and great array, borne in their gilded kago. The night fell.

"I lose sweet hope," said Urashima,

But there passed by an old, old man.

"Oh, old, old man," cried the fisherman, "you have seen many days; know you aught of Urashima? In this place was he born and bred."

Then the old man said, "There was one of that name, but, sir, that one was drowned long years ago. My grandfather could scarce remember him in the time that I was a little boy. Good stranger, it was many, many years ago."

Urashima said, "He is dead?"

"No man more dead than he. His sons are dead and their sons are dead. Good even to you, stranger."

Then Urashima was afraid. But he said, "I must go to the green valley where the dead sleep." And to the valley he took his way.

He said, "How chill the night wind blows through the grass! The trees shiver and the leaves turn their pale backs to me."

He said, "Hail, sad moon, that showest me all the quiet graves. Thou art nothing different from the moon of old."

He said, "Here are my sons' graves and their sons' graves. Poor Urashima, there is no man more dead than he. Yet am I lonely among the ghosts."

"Who will comfort me?" said Urashima.

The night wind sighed and nothing more.

Then he went back to the seashore. "Who will comfort me?" cried Urashima. But the sky was unmoved, and the mountain waves of the sea rolled on.

Urashima said, "There is the casket." And he took it from his sleeve and opened it. There rose from it a faint white smoke that floated away and out to the far horizon.

"I grow very weary," said Urashima. In a moment his hair turned as white as snow. He trembled, his body shrank, his eyes grew dim. He that had been so young and lusty swayed and tottered where he stood.

"I am old," said Urashima,

He made to shut the casket lid, but dropped it, saying, "Nay, the vapor of smoke is gone forever. What matters it?"

He laid down his length upon the sand and died.

ROKUROKUBI

Nearly five hundred years ago there was a samurai, named Isogai Hei-dazaemon Taketsura, in the service of the Lord Kikuji, of Kyushu. This Isogai had inherited, from many warlike ancestors, a natural aptitude for military exercises, and extraordinary strength. While yet a boy he had surpassed his teachers in the art of swordsmanship, in archery, and in the use of the spear, and had displayed all the capacities of a daring and skillful soldier. Afterwards, in the time of the Eikyo[1] war, he so distinguished himself that high honors were bestowed upon him. But when the house of Kikuji came to ruin, Isogai found himself without a master. He might then easily have obtained service under another daimyo; but as he had never sought distinction for his own sake alone, and as his heart remained true to his former lord, he preferred to give up the world. So he cut off his hair, and became a traveling priest, taking the Buddhist name of Kwairyo.

But always, under the *koromo*[2] of the priest, Kwairyo kept warm within him the heart of the samurai. As in other years he had laughed at peril, so now also he scorned danger; and in all weathers and all seasons he journeyed to preach the good Law in places where no other priest would have dared to go. For that age was an age of violence and disorder; and upon the highways there was no security for the solitary traveler, even if he happened to be a priest.

In the course of his first long journey, Kwairyo had occasion to visit the province of Kai.[3] One evening, as he was traveling through the mountains of that province, darkness overcame him in a very lonesome district, leagues away from any village. So he resigned himself to pass the night under the stars; and having found a suitable grassy spot, by the roadside, he lay down there, and prepared to sleep. He had always welcomed discomfort; and even a bare rock was for him a good bed, when nothing better could be found, and the root of a pine tree an excellent pillow. His body was iron; and he never troubled himself about dews or rain or frost or snow.

Scarcely had he lain down when a man came along the road, carrying an ax and a great bundle of chopped wood. This woodcutter halted on seeing Kwairyo lying down, and, after a moment of silent observation, said to him in a tone of great surprise:

"What kind of a man can you be, good Sir, that you dare to lie down alone in such a place as this? There are haunters about here—many of them. Are you not afraid of Hairy Things?"

"My friend," cheerfully answered Kwairyo, "I am only a wandering priest—a 'Cloud-and-Water-Guest,' as folks call it: *Unsui-no-ryokaku*.[4] And I am not in the least afraid of Hairy Things—if you mean goblin-foxes, or goblin-badgers, or any creatures of that kind. As for lonesome places, I like them: they are suitable for meditation. I am accustomed to sleeping in the open air: and I have learned never to be anxious about my life."

"You must be indeed a brave man, Sir Priest," the peasant responded, "to lie down here! This place has a bad name—a very bad name. But, as the proverb has it, *Kunshi ayayuki ni chikayorazu* ['The superior man does not needlessly expose himself to peril']; and I must assure you, Sir, that it is very dangerous to sleep here. Therefore, although my house is only a wretched thatched hut, let me beg of you to come home with me at once. In the way of food, I have nothing to offer you; but there is a roof at least, and you can sleep under it without risk."

He spoke earnestly; and Kwairyo, liking the kindly tone of the man, accepted this modest offer. The woodcutter guided him along a narrow path, leading up from the main road through mountain-forest. It was a rough and danger-ous path—sometimes skirting precipices, sometimes offering nothing but a network of slippery roots for the foot to rest upon, sometimes winding over or between masses of jagged rock. But at last Kwairyo found himself upon a cleared space at the top of a hill, with a full moon shining overhead; and he saw before him a small thatched cottage, cheerfully lighted from within. The woodcutter led him to a shed at the back of the house, whither water had been conducted, through bamboo pipes, from some neighboring stream; and the two men washed their feet. Beyond the shed was a vegetable garden, and a grove of cedars and bamboos; and beyond the trees appeared the glimmer of a cascade, pouring from some loftier height, and swaying in the moonshine like a long white robe.

As Kwairyo entered the cottage with his guide, he perceived four persons—men and women—warming their hands at a little fire kindled in the *ro*[5] of the principal apartment. They bowed low to the priest, and greeted him in the most respectful manner. Kwairyo wondered that persons so poor, and dwell-ing in such a solitude, should be aware of the polite forms of greeting. "These are good people," he thought to himself; "and they must have been taught by someone well acquainted with the rules of propriety." Then turning to his host—the *aruji*, or house-master, as the others called him—Kwairyo said:

"From the kindness of your speech, and from the very polite welcome given me by your household, I imagine that you have not always been a woodcutter. Perhaps you formerly belonged to one of the upper classes?"

Smiling, the woodcutter answered:

"Sir, you are not mistaken. Though now living as you find me, I was once a person of some distinction. My story is the story of a ruined life—ruined by my own fault. I used to be in the service of a daimyo; and my rank in that service was not inconsiderable. But I loved women and wine too well; and under the influence of passion I acted wickedly. My selfishness brought about the ruin of our house, and caused the death of many persons. Retribution followed me; and I long remained a fugitive in the land. Now I often pray that I may be able to make some atonement for the evil which I did, and to reestablish the ancestral home. But I fear that I shall never find any way of so doing. Never-theless, I try to overcome the karma of my errors by sincere repentance, and by helping, as far as I can, those who are unfortunate."

Kwairyo was pleased by this announcement of good resolve; and he said to the *aruji*:

"My friend, I have had occasion to observe that men, prone to folly in their youth, may in after years become very earnest in right living. In the holy sutras it is written that those strongest in wrong-doing can become, by power of good resolve, the strongest in right-doing. I do not doubt that you have a good heart; and I hope that better fortune will come to you. Tonight I shall recite the sutras for your sake, and pray that you may obtain the force to overcome the karma of any past errors."

With these assurances, Kwairyo bade the *aruji* goodnight; and his host showed him to a very small side room, where a bed had been made ready. Then all went to sleep except the priest, who began to read the sutras by the light of a paper lantern. Until a late hour he continued to read and pray: then he opened a little window in his little sleeping-room, to take a last look at the landscape before lying down. The night was beautiful: there was no cloud in the sky: there was no wind; and the strong moonlight threw down sharp black shadows of foliage, and glittered on the dews of the garden. Shrillings of crickets and bell-insects[6] made a musical tumult; and the sound of the neighboring cascade deepened with the night. Kwairyo felt thirsty as he listened to the noise of the water; and, remembering the bamboo aqueduct at the rear of the house, he thought that he could go there and get a drink without disturbing the sleeping household. Very gently he pushed apart the sliding screens that separated his room from the main apartment; and he saw, by the light of the lantern, five recumbent bodies—without heads!

For one instant he stood bewildered, imagining a crime. But in another moment he perceived that there was no blood, and that the headless necks did not look as if they had been cut. Then he thought to himself: "Either this is an illusion made by goblins, or I have been lured into the dwelling of a Rokurokubi...[7] In the book *Soshinki*[8] it is written that if one should find the body of a Rokurokubi without its head, and remove the body to another place, the head will never be able to join itself again to the neck. And the book further says that when the head comes back and finds that its body has been moved, it will strike itself upon the floor three times, bounding like a ball, and will pant as in great fear, and presently die. Now, if these be Rokurokubi, they mean me no good; so I shall be justified in following the instructions of the book."

He seized the body of the *aruji* by the feet, pulled it to the window, and pushed it out. Then he went to the back door, which he found barred; and he surmised that the heads had made their exit through the smoke-hole in the roof, which had been left open. Gently unbarring the door, he made his way to the garden, and proceeded with all possible caution to the grove beyond it. He heard voices talking in the grove; and he went in the direction of the voices, stealing from shadow to shadow, until he reached a good hiding place. Then, from behind a trunk, he caught sight of the heads—all five of them—flitting about, and chatting as they flitted. They were eating worms and insects which they found on the ground or among the trees. Presently the head of the *aruji* stopped eating and said:

"Ah, that traveling priest who came tonight! How fat all his body is! When we shall have eaten him, our bellies will be well filled… I was foolish to talk to him as I did; it only set him to reciting the sutras on behalf of my soul! To go near him while he is reciting would be difficult; and we cannot touch him so long as he is praying. But as it is now nearly morning, perhaps he has gone to sleep… Some one of you go to the house and see what the fellow is doing."

Another head—the head of a young woman—immediately rose up and flitted to the house, lightly as a bat. After a few minutes it came back, and cried out huskily, in a tone of great alarm:

"That traveling priest is not in the house—he is gone! But that is not the worst of the matter. He has taken the body of our *aruji*; and I do not know where he has put it."

At this announcement the head of the *aruji*—distinctly visible in the moonlight—assumed a frightful aspect: its eyes opened monstrously; its hair stood up bristling; and its teeth gnashed. Then a cry burst from its lips; and—weeping tears of rage—it exclaimed:

"Since my body has been moved, to rejoin it is not possible! Then I must die! And all through the work of that priest! Before I die I will get at that priest! I will tear him! I will devour him! *And there he is*—behind that tree! Hiding behind that tree! See him—the fat coward!"

In the same moment the head of the *aruji*, followed by the other four heads, sprang at Kwairyo. But the strong priest had already armed himself by plucking up a young tree; and with that tree he struck the heads as they came, knocking them from him with tremendous blows. Four of them fled away. But the head of the *aruji*, though battered again and again, desperately continued to bound at the priest, and at last caught him by the left sleeve of his robe. Kwairyo, however, as quickly gripped the head by its topknot, and repeatedly struck it. It did not release its hold; but it uttered a long moan, and thereafter ceased to struggle. It was dead. But its teeth still held the sleeve; and, for all his great strength, Kwairyo could not force open the jaws.

With the head still hanging to his sleeve he went back to the house, and there caught sight of the other four Rokurokubi squatting together, with their bruised and bleeding heads reunited to their bodies. But when they perceived him at the back door all screamed, "The priest! the priest!" and fled, through the other doorway, out into the woods.

Eastward the sky was brightening; day was about to dawn; and Kwairyo knew that the power of the goblins was limited to the hours of darkness. He looked at the head clinging to his sleeve, its face all fouled with blood and foam and clay; and he laughed aloud as he thought to himself: "What a *miyage*[9]—the head of a goblin!" After which he gathered together his few belongings, and leisurely descended the mountain to continue his journey.

Right on he journeyed, until he came to Suwa in Shinano;[10] and into the main street of Suwa he solemnly strode, with the head dangling at his elbow. Then women fainted, and children screamed and ran away; and there was a great crowding and clamoring until the *torite* (as the police in those days were called) seized the priest, and took him to jail. For they supposed the head to be the head of a murdered man who, in the moment of being killed, had caught the murderer's sleeve in his teeth. As for Kwairyo, he only smiled and said nothing when they questioned him. So, after having passed a night in prison, he was brought before the magistrates of the district. Then he was ordered to explain how he, a priest, had been found with the head of a man fastened to his sleeve, and why he had dared thus shamelessly to parade his crime in the sight of people.

Kwairyo laughed long and loudly at these questions; and then he said:

"Sirs, I did not fasten the head to my sleeve: it fastened itself there—much against my will. And I have not committed any crime. For this is not the head of a man; it is the head of a goblin; and, if I caused the death of the goblin, I did not do so by any shedding of blood, but simply by taking the precautions necessary to assure my own safety." And he proceeded to relate the whole of the adventure, bursting into another hearty laugh as he told of his encounter with the five heads.

But the magistrates did not laugh. They judged him to be a hardened criminal, and his story an insult to their intelligence. Therefore, without further questioning, they decided to order his immediate execution—all of them except one, a very old man. This aged officer had made no remark during the trial; but, after having heard the opinion of his colleagues, he rose up, and said:

"Let us first examine the head carefully; for this, I think, has not yet been done. If the priest has spoken truth, the head itself should bear witness for him... Bring the head here!"

So the head, still holding in its teeth the *koromo* that had been stripped from Kwairyo's shoulders, was put before the judges. The old man turned it round and round, carefully examined it, and discovered, on the nape of its neck, several strange red characters. He called the attention of his colleagues to these, and also bade them observe that the edges of the neck nowhere presented the appearance of having been cut by any weapon. On the contrary, the line of leverance was smooth as the line at which a falling leaf detaches itself from the stem... Then said the elder:

"I am quite sure that the priest told us nothing but the truth. This is the head of a Rokurokubi. In the book *Nan-ho-i-butsu-shi* it is written that certain red characters can always be found upon the nape of the neck of a real Rokuro-kubi. There are the characters: you can see for yourselves that they have not been painted. Moreover, it is well known that such goblins have been dwelling in the mountains of the province of Kai from very ancient time... But you, Sir," he exclaimed, turning to Kwairyo, "what sort of sturdy priest may you be? Certainly you have given proof of a courage that few priests possess; and you have the air of a soldier rather than a priest. Perhaps you once belonged to the samurai class?"

"You have guessed rightly, Sir," Kwairyo responded. "Before becoming a priest, I long followed the profession of arms; and in those days I never feared man or devil. My name then was Isogai Heidazaemon Taketsura of Kyushu: there may be some among you who remember it."

At the mention of that name, a murmur of admiration filled the court-room; for there were many present who remembered it. And Kwairyo immediately found himself among friends instead of judges—friends anxious to prove their admiration by fraternal kindness. With honor they escorted him to the residence of the daimyo, who welcomed him, and feasted him, and made him a handsome present before allowing him to depart. When Kwairyo left Suwa, he was as happy as any priest is permitted to be in this transitory world. As for the head, he took it with him—jocosely insisting that he intended it for a *miyage*.

And now it only remains to tell what became of the head.

A day or two after leaving Suwa, Kwairyo met with a robber, who stopped him in a lonesome place, and bade him strip. Kwairyo at once removed his *koromo*, and offered it to the robber, who then first perceived what was hanging to the sleeve. Though brave, the highwayman was startled: he dropped the garment, and sprang back. Then he cried out: "You! What kind of a priest are you? Why, you are a worse man than I am! It is true that I have killed people; but I never walked about with anybody's head fastened to my sleeve... Well, Sir priest, I suppose we are of the same calling; and I must say that I admire you! Now that head would be of use to me: I could frighten people with it. Will you sell it? You can have my robe in exchange for your *koromo*; and I will give you five *ryo* for the head."

Kwairyo answered:

"I shall let you have the head and the robe if you insist; but I must tell you that this is not the head of a man. It is a goblin's head. So, if you buy it, and have any trouble in consequence, please to remember that you were not deceived by me."

"What a nice priest you are!" exclaimed the robber. "You kill men, and jest about it! But I am really in earnest. Here is my robe; and here is the money; and let me have the head... What is the use of joking?"

"Take the thing," said Kwairyo. "I was not joking. The only joke—if there be any joke at all—is that you are fool enough to pay good money for a goblin's head." And Kwairyo, loudly laughing, went upon his way.

Thus the robber got the head and the *koromo*; and for some time he played goblin-priest upon the highways. But, reaching the neighborhood of Suwa, he there learned the true story of the head; and he then became afraid that the spirit of the Rokurokubi might give him trouble. So he made up his mind to take back the head to the place from which it had come, and to bury it with its body. He found his way to the lonely cottage in the mountains of Kai; but nobody was there, and he could not discover the body. Therefore he buried the head by itself, in the grove behind the cottage; and he had a tombstone set up over the grave; and he caused a *segaki* service to be performed on behalf of the spirit of the Rokurokubi. And that tombstone—known as the Tombstone of the Rokurokubi—may be seen (at least so the Japanese storyteller declares) even unto this day.

Notes

1. The period of Eikyo lasted from 1429 to 1441.
2. The upper robe of a Buddhist priest is thus called.
3. Present-day Yamanashi Prefecture.
4. A term for itinerant priests.
5. A sort of little fireplace, contrived in the floor of a room, is thus described. The *ro* is usually a square shallow cavity, lined with metal and half-filled with ashes, in which charcoal is lighted.
6. Direct translation of *suzumushi*, a kind of cricket with a distinctive chirp like a tiny bell, whence the name.
7. Now a Rokurokubi is ordinarily conceived as a goblin whose neck stretches out to great lengths, but which nevertheless always remains attached to its body.
8. A Chinese collection of stories on the supernatural.
9. A present made to friends or to the household on returning from a journey is thus called. Ordinarily, of course, the *miyage* consists of something produced in the locality to which the journey has been made: this is the point of Kwairyo's jest.
10. Present-day Nagano Prefecture.

FRAGMENT

And it was at the hour of sunset that they came to the foot of the mountain. There was in that place no sign of life—neither token of water, nor trace of plant, nor shadow of flying bird—nothing but desolation rising to desolation. And the summit was lost in heaven.

Then the Bodhisattva said to his young companion: "What you have asked to see will be shown to you. But the place of the Vision is far; and the way is rude. Follow after me, and do not fear: strength will be given you."

Twilight gloomed about them as they climbed. There was no beaten path, nor any mark of former human visitation; and the way was over an endless heaping of tumbled fragments that rolled or turned beneath the foot. Sometimes a mass dislodged would clatter down with hollow echoings; sometimes the substance trodden would burst like an empty shell... Stars pointed and thrilled; and the darkness deepened.

"Do not fear, my son," said the Bodhisattva, guiding: "danger there is none, though the way be grim."

Under the stars they climbed—fast, fast—mounting by help of power super-human. High zones of mist they passed; and they saw below them, ever widening as they climbed, a soundless flood of cloud, like the tide of a milky sea.

Hour after hour they climbed; and forms invisible yielded to their tread with dull soft crashings; and faint cold fires lighted and died at every breaking.

And once the pilgrim-youth laid hand on a something smooth that was not stone—and lifted it—and dimly saw the cheekless gibe of death.

"Linger not thus, my son!" urged the voice of the teacher, "the summit that we must gain is very far away!"

On through the dark they climbed—and felt continually beneath them the soft strange breakings—and saw the icy fires worm and die—till the rim of the night turned gray, and the stars began to fail, and the east began to bloom.

Yet still they climbed—fast, fast—mounting by help of power superhuman. About them now was frigidness of death—and silence tremendous... A gold flame kindled in the east.

Then first to the pilgrim's gaze the steeps revealed their nakedness—and a trembling seized him—and a ghastly fear. For there was not any ground—neither beneath him nor about him nor above him—but a heaping only, monstrous and measureless, of skulls and fragments of skulls and dust of bone—with a shimmer of shed teeth strown through the drift of it, like the shimmer of scrags of shell in the wrack of a tide.

"Do not fear, my son!" cried the voice of the Bodhisattva; "only the strong of heart can win to the place of the Vision!"

Behind them the world had vanished. Nothing remained but the clouds beneath, and the sky above, and the heaping of skulls between—up-slanting out of sight.

Then the sun climbed with the climbers; and there was no warmth in the light of him, but coldness sharp as a sword. And the horror of stupendous height, and the nightmare of stupendous depth, and the terror of silence, ever grew and grew, and weighed upon the pilgrim, and held his feet—so that suddenly all power departed from him, and he moaned like a sleeper in dreams.

"Hasten, hasten, my son!" cried the Bodhisattva: "the day is brief, and the summit is very far away."

But the pilgrim shrieked—"I fear! I fear unspeakably!—and the power has departed from me!"

"The power will return, my son," made answer the Bodhisattva.... "Look now below you and above you and about you, and tell me what you see."

"I cannot," cried the pilgrim, trembling and clinging; "I dare not look beneath! Before me and about me there is nothing but skulls of men."

"And yet, my son," said the Bodhisattva, laughing softly, "and yet you do not know of what this mountain is made."

The other, shuddering, repeated: "I fear—unutterably I fear! ...There is nothing but skulls of men!"

"A mountain of skulls it is," responded the Bodhisattva. "But know, my son, that all of them ARE YOUR OWN! Each has at some time been the nest of your dreams and delusions and desires. Not even one of them is the skull of any other being. All—all without exception—have been yours, in the billions of your former lives."

Publisher's Note

The stories in this volume are drawn from six books by Lafcadio Hearn and Yei Theodora Ozaki, two great interpreters of Japanese culture during the early twentieth century. Hearn was born in Greece and lived in Ireland and the United States before coming to Japan at the age of forty, where he married a samurai's daughter and became a Japanese citizen. Ozaki was born to an English mother and a Japanese father and grew up in both countries, later traveling in Europe for several years before settling in Japan and marrying the mayor of Tokyo. Hearn went on to publish fourteen books about Japan, and Ozaki four. Although their writing styles are distinct, they shared a gift for storytelling and a multicultural perspective that allowed them to not simply translate the legends, ghost stories and fairy tales of Japan but rather to retell them in a way that captured—and continues to capture—the imaginations of Western readers. Ozaki writes in the preface to *Japanese Fairy Tales*, her first book, that her stories "are not literal translations." Instead, she continues, "I have followed my fancy in adding such touches of local color or description as they seemed to need or as pleased me." In this she follows a long tradition of storytellers around the world who have made classic tales their own. Hearn, too, brings his inimitable voice to retellings of stories gleaned from old Japanese books and other sources, writing in the introduction to "A Passional Karma," for instance, that he "tried to keep close to the [original Japanese] text only in the conversational passages." Both authors filter "old Japan" through an international lens, but always with deep affection for and interest in the traditions they draw on.

The source of each story is listed in the following pages. Wherever possible, the Japanese sources that Hearn and Ozaki worked from are also noted, but often this information was not available. We are indebted to the many unnamed Japanese writers and storytellers who kept alive the tales in this book so that another generation can enjoy them.

Sources

The Story of Mimi Nashi Hoichi
From *Kwaidan* by Lafcadio Hearn (1904).

How an Old Man Lost His Wen
From *Japanese Fairy Tales* by Yei Theodora Ozaki (1908).
Based on a version of the story by Sadanami Sanjin.

The Boy Who Drew Cats
From *Japanese Fairy Tales* by Lafcadio Hearn and Others (1918).

The Badger Haunted Temple
From *Romances of Old Japan* by Yei Theodora Ozaki (1920).

The Story of the Man Who Did Not Wish to Die
From *Japanese Fairy Tales* by Yei Theodora Ozaki (1908).
Based on a story by Shunsui Tamenaga.

The Spirit of the Lantern
From *Romances of Old Japan* by Yei Theodora Ozaki (1920).

The Serpent with Eight Heads
From *Japanese Fairy Tales* by Lafcadio Hearn and Others (1918).
Based on the Yamata no Orochi legend, first recorded in the Kojiki and Nihon
  Shoki.
The translator of the version in *Japanese Fairy Tales* is not specified.

A Passional Karma
From *In Ghostly Japan* by Lafcadio Hearn (1899).
Based on *Kaidan botan doro* by Sanyutei Encho.

The Bamboo Cutter and the Moon Child

From *Japanese Fairy Tales* by Yei Theodora Ozaki (1908).
Based on *Taketori monogatari*, a tenth-century narrative by an unknown author.

The Goblin of Oeyama

From *Warriors of Old Japan and Other Stories* by Yei Theodora Ozaki (1909).

Kidomaru the Robber, Raiko the Brave, and the Goblin Spider

From *Warriors of Old Japan and Other Stories* by Yei Theodora Ozaki (1909).

A Cherry Flower Idyll

From *Romances of Old Japan* by Yei Theodora Ozaki (1920).

Urashima

From *Japanese Fairy Tales* by Lafcadio Hearn and Others (1918).
Based on the legend of Urashimako, first recorded in the 8th century.
The translator of the version in *Japanese Fairy Tales* is not specified.

Rokurokubi

From *Kwaidan* by Lafcadio Hearn (1904).

Fragment

From *In Ghostly Japan* by Lafcadio Hearn (1899).

"Books to Span the East and West"

Tuttle Publishing was founded in 1832 in the small New England town of Rutland, Vermont [USA]. Our core values remain as strong today as they were then—to publish best-in-class books which bring people together one page at a time. In 1948, we established a publishing outpost in Japan—and Tuttle is now a leader in publishing English-language books about the arts, languages and cultures of Asia. The world has become a much smaller place today and Asia's economic and cultural influence has grown. Yet the need for meaningful dialogue and information about this diverse region has never been greater. Over the past seven decades, Tuttle has published thousands of books on subjects ranging from martial arts and paper crafts to language learning and literature—and our talented authors, illustrators, designers and photographers have won many prestigious awards. We welcome you to explore the wealth of information available on Asia at www.tuttlepublishing.com.

Published by Tuttle Publishing, an imprint of Periplus Editions (HK) Ltd.

www.tuttlepublishing.com

Copyright © 2024 Periplus Editions (HK) Ltd.
Illustrations © 2024 Hana Tottori

Library of Congress Control Number: 2024934531

ISBN 978-4-8053-1853-9

First edition
28 27 26 25 24
10 9 8 7 6 5 4 3 2 1   2405EP
Printed in China

TUTTLE PUBLISHING® is a registered trademark of Tuttle Publishing, a division of Periplus Editions (HK) Ltd.

Distributed by

North America, Latin America & Europe
Tuttle Publishing
364 Innovation Drive, North Clarendon
VT 05759-9436 U.S.A.
Tel: 1 (802) 773-8930
Fax: 1 (802) 773-6993
info@tuttlepublishing.com
www.tuttlepublishing.com

Japan
Tuttle Publishing
Yaekari Building 3rd Floor
5-4-12 Osaki Shinagawa-ku
Tokyo 141 0032
Tel: (81) 3 5437-0171
Fax: (81) 3 5437-0755
sales@tuttle.co.jp
www.tuttle.co.jp

Asia Pacific
Berkeley Books Pte. Ltd.
3 Kallang Sector #04-01
Singapore 349278
Tel: (65) 6741-2178
Fax: (65) 6741-2179
inquiries@periplus.com.sg
www.tuttlepublishing.com